THIRTY-EIGHT DAYS OF RAIN

Eva Asprakis

For J

MARCH

The Second

Rain hammers at the window as Androulla hoists herself up onto the examination table. It spans the wall of a utilitarian office above Makarios Avenue, a street vibrant with swimwear shops and, now, girls shrieking to escape the weather. The window rattles. Turning her head, Androulla notes that its sill could do with a clean.

"We'll check everything," the doctor says, brandishing his transducer, "to be sure. Lay back."

Androulla draws her knees up. The paper towel shifts up the table with her, and she leans forward to straighten it. As though oblivious, the doctor advances. Androulla stammers apologies as she fumbles with her zip. She didn't know, when she pulled on her jeans this morning, that she would be shimmying out of them on her back. If she had, she might have worn looser trousers. Or accepted her mother's offer to accompany her to this appointment.

"For all the cowboys they have here," Olympia had muttered, this morning.

"Lift up," the doctor says.

Olympia is wrong about Cyprus, Androulla tells herself as she pulls up her top. Her first short sleeve of the year. The rain comes harder at the window.

"Up," the doctor repeats, exposing the band of Androulla's bra.

Her cheeks warm to a matching red. Before she can ask the doctor what he is doing, why he needs to see her undressed, he spurts cold gel onto her stomach.

"Relax."

"Sorry. It tickles," she says, as her gasp gives way to a giggle.

He is rubbing the gel around her stomach with the nose of the transducer, making her tense up.

"Relax," he says again, this time looking away.

She follows his gaze along the wire to a hulking grey machine. On top of it, a screen echoes her insides in black-and-white. She turns her eyes up to the ceiling, commanding her body to soften as the transducer digs deeper into her abdomen. Her bladder cries out, sharply.

"Okay," the doctor murmurs.

Androulla catches the scent of coffee on his breath. The pressure moves higher up her torso, over her belly button and ribs. As he comes to her breasts, she stills. She takes in his grey stubble and his sun-ripened skin, the rectangular lenses through which he is staring back at her. The cold creeps over her chest before he retracts his transducer.

"Turn your head," he says.

Heart thudding, she looks to the window. It is a panel of grey, a rare sight in Cyprus. Androulla wills the rain to wash away her discomfort as the pressure returns to her neck. This is it, she thinks. The doctor pauses over the lump that she has been prodding for days. It isn't a visible protrusion, but one that she felt as she rubbed at the base of her neck. A hardened ball, about the size of a pea, that slid out from under her finger like it didn't want to be discovered. Not until it had grown, Androulla feared, into something larger and altogether more sinister.

The doctor lets out a grunt. She looks sideways at him. He is leaning closer to the screen, pressing harder at her neck until the growth catches and she whimpers.

"Turn on the other side," he instructs her, pulling back.

Androulla does as he says. "Am I okay?" she asks, in a voice made small by the weight upon her windpipe.

The doctor keeps his lips pressed firm until the machine gives him an invisible sign.

Finally, he lifts her right forearm. "Where was the previous cyst?" he asks.

She points to the pink-white scar beneath her elbow, grimacing at its tenderness under the transducer. Then she exhales.

"Okay," the doctor says, as he hangs it up. He hands her a wad of tissue thinner than kitchen roll. "Clean yourself, and we'll see the results."

Wiping the gel off her stomach, Androulla casts the tissue into a corner bin. Her skin still feels slick as she pulls up her jeans, but she doesn't want to ask the doctor for more. He is sitting at another screen when she rounds the corner, indicating a seat across his desk. She takes it, pulsing her leg up and down and surveying the room. Another, larger window with the rain streaking down it. Dark wooden shelves of anatomical models, and books whose titles she cannot focus on.

"I had another cyst, like, ten years ago? When I was fourteen," she says, to break the silence. "It was on one of my ovaries, and it ruptured . . ."

"Yes," the doctor says, without looking up from his computer. "You have polycystic ovaries."

With a 'click', the mouse gives way beneath his finger, a printer wheezes into action and he crosses the room. Androulla blinks.

"This is your scan," the doctor says, sliding a sonogram across the desk as he resumes his seat. "All healthy. There is just one swollen lymph node in your neck."

Androulla searches the image. "Is that bad?" she asks, looking up at the doctor.

He waves a hand. "This is a benign situation. Probably, it's because of your acne."

Her hands rise to her jaw.

"And your acne, probably, is because of your polycystic ovaries. Don't worry about this." He reaches for a notepad and pen. "I'll write you some pills to help with your skin. They're one-hundred percent natural, no chemicals. You'll see a lot of improvement."

"Right," Androulla says. She lowers her hands. "Sorry, so polycystic ovaries. What is that?"

At the bottom of his page, the doctor signs off with a loose scribble. "You have irregular periods?"

"Sometimes," she admits.

"This is polycystic ovaries. You have a lot of scarring, you can see here," he says, with a nod towards her scan. "It's a common condition which affects the function of the ovaries. You have to take care of them with your diet. No sugar, no carbs. Because you see, with these," he says, indicating one of several dark patches, "you will never catch a baby."

There is a thud as he stamps his page, then tears it off and holds it out to her.

"Okay? You can find these pills in any pharmacy. I want you to take two per day, and in six weeks we'll see how your lymph node is going on."

The paper feels like nothing between Androulla's fingers.

"Thank you," she says, folding it into her tote bag.

"*Geiá sas*," the doctor bids her, sitting back.

It is only as she is settling up with his receptionist, wincing, that Androulla realises they have been speaking in English. Despite her Greek-speaking parents and the year that she has lived in Cyprus, she shies away from technical language. Anything medical, or legal. This is happening more often, as if to secure her status as a Cypriot she must first regress from her strong start of ordering in coffee shops and exchanging anecdotes with her stepfather. She drifts down the stairs of the doctor's office to the car park, where no one has stopped inside the lines and the rain is falling, steadily. She forgets it slicking down her back as she walks the twenty minutes home to her apartment.

"Oh," Giannis says, when he opens the door. He stands back to watch her drip onto the mat. "I told you, you should have worn a jacket."

"Mmn hmn," Androulla says, kicking off her trainers. She lifts them over the threshold, pulling the door shut behind her.

"Hi, Wife," Giannis says, as he takes her into his arms.

"Hi, Wife," she mimics, into his chest.

Despite his familiar chuckle and his old scent like eucalyptus, it is still strange to hear. Wife. He hasn't stopped addressing her this way in the three weeks since their wedding, as if she has lost her first name despite not taking his second. She is not Androulla anymore, but *gynaíka*.

"How was that?" Giannis asks, drawing back to look at her. He stops his fingers just short of the growth on her neck. "Did you find out, what . . ?"

She pulls her t-shirt unstuck from her chest. "It's a swollen lymph node, which is a result of my spots. Which," she goes on, rolling her eyes at the frown he pulls, "are a result of my polycystic ovaries."

"Right," he says, lowering his hand. "What does that mean?"

"It means," Androulla says, with a long breath out, "I can't have kids."

Beyond the window, the rain pummels on. She studies her husband's brown eyes, his long lashes, the wrinkle of his nose before his eyebrows part.

"You can't have kids," he repeats, with his Australian twang. "At all?"

She lowers her bag to the floor. "It's highly unlikely, with the scarring on my ovaries."

They stare at each other, until a grin overcomes Giannis's face.

"Do you know how much money we're going to save?"

Androulla falls back a step, laughing.

"Honestly, the price of condoms . . ."

"I know. It's ridiculous."

"And the rate we get through them . . ."

"Plus it is just, better, without."

Giannis claps his hands and the sound echoes through their apartment, with its close walls and hard-tiled floors. Androulla gives another laugh and tucks her hair back, cold.

Giannis drops his arms to ask, "You're not upset by this, are you?"

"No," she assures him, mirroring the movement. "I mean, it was shocking to hear. But I guess that's natural, isn't it? Even though we've never wanted to . . ." She lets her shoulders sink down from a shrug.

Nodding, Giannis takes hold of them. "I'd understand if you were upset, though. I'd want to support you," he says.

"Thanks," Androulla mumbles.

"You would tell me, wouldn't you?" he says, squeezing her arms.

She restores her smile. "You know I would. Maybe I need more time to digest it, I don't know. But for now, I'm excited," she says, turning the top button of his shirt between her finger and thumb.

"Hmn," Giannis purrs, tilting his face down to meet hers.

Androulla plucks the button loose with her right hand, placing her left upon his chest to display her new ring. A gold band, stacked above the emerald that she has worn for three years. She relishes the warmth of her husband's lips and the scratch of his shadow across her chin, her need to crane on her tiptoes to reach him, though he is barely five-foot-seven. He slides his hand down her back and she pulls away.

"Does that make me a bad woman?" she asks.

Giannis's eyes flicker. "I hope so," he says.

Androulla's t-shirt thuds to the floor. They fall into bed, Giannis flinching at Androulla's cold touch. He arches away from her as he lets out a final moan.

"Fuck," he breathes into her ear, before he kisses it.

She laughs, rolling to her feet. "I'll be back in a minute."

The bathroom light makes her squint after the darkness of their bedroom. She uses paper to dry herself, just as she did at the doctor's, then stands and faces the mirror. It has a crack in one corner, and flecks of toothpaste from where they brush their teeth. Androulla studies her reflection, her blemished skin and her full lips, the mascara rubbed around her heavy-lidded brown eyes. Semi-circular breasts, arms never as thin as she thinks they should be, though their flesh springs straight back when she pinches it. The breath sags from her lungs. For all the times she has come into her palm, watching the fluid drip from between the legs of a girl online, there is something anticlimactic about the experience. Something that leaves Androulla feeling hollow as she pads back to bed, and Giannis turns off the lamp.

"I love you," he says.

"I love you too," she murmurs.

The Sixth

AT THE SOUND OF footsteps, Androulla looks up. They are the block-heeled thuds of a woman just over the hilltop of forty, red-cheeked as though from her climb. She has crossed the square hallway twice already. Androulla smiled at her the first time, feeling a peak of anticipation in her stomach, before the woman marched on with her armful of documents. She isn't the one. And yet Androulla sits with her head bowed just so, hands folded in her lap as her primary school teachers used to tell her. She could be in a classroom here, with the felt-tip drawings of houses and families pinned to rectangular boards in place of windows, and a bead maze looping the loop. Androulla's mother is perched on the bench beside her, with her signature scent of jasmine. A pace away, her stepfather stands, crossing and uncrossing his arms.

A door marked '*Psychológos*' creaks open.

"Androulla Dixon?" a long-haired woman asks, stepping out.

Androulla gives her a bright nod.

Returning it, the psychologist looks down at her clipboard. "So you are Olympia Demetriou, her mother?"

"Yes," Olympia says.

"And Kostas Demetriou, her stepfather?"

"Nice to meet you," Kostas says, with a nervous laugh. "Good morning."

Androulla bristles. Her stepfather has always made awkward introductions – to her teachers at Parents' Evening and to Giannis's parents at their wedding – as though hyperaware of his adjunct position. Except when he presents Androulla to colleagues and cashiers, people who skim across the surface of their lives without diving deeper. This is my daughter, he says then, making her smile. She glances up at a 'Family Court' sign.

"Annita," the psychologist introduces herself, lowering her clipboard. "So, who wants to go first?"

They look at each other.

"I will," Olympia says.

Androulla watches her disappear behind the door of Annita's office, short as ever in her white trousers and embroidered top, as if the importance of this moment has weighed upon her shoulders for years. The bench creaks as Kostas takes her place. Androulla shifts sideways, away from and then towards him as the block-heeled woman reappears.

"What do you think she'll ask about?" Androulla asks, under her breath.

With his eyes fixed to the floor, Kostas shakes his head.

Another door swings open and Androulla clamps down on her tongue. When the quiet resumes, she hears the low murmur of her mother's voice.

"Do you think she'll try to catch us out?" she asks.

Kostas glances sideways, then says, "She can't catch us out because we're telling the truth, right? Except about Giannis."

Androulla looks at her stepfather, his full beard and his thinning hair, his skin like gold against the pink shirt that he has worn for this occasion. Its paleness touches her in contrast to his 'uniform' of black t-shirts and cargo shorts. She nods. The block-heeled woman stalks past them twice more.

Then, from the doorway, Olympia calls, "Kosta."

Without a word, Kostas springs up and catches the door. He bends to kiss her before it bumps shut behind him. In a mist of jasmine, Olympia sits back down.

"How was that?" Androulla asks her.

"Good," Olympia says, arranging her bag strap across her lap.

"You were ages."

"Was I?"

Androulla stares at her. "Well," she says, "what did you talk about?"

Olympia crosses her right knee over her left. "We talked about what you were like as a child. The first time you met Kostas, when you brought him a book and climbed onto his lap."

"Jonah and the Whale," Androulla smiles. "I remember."

Olympia frowns. "You were very young."

"I remember the book, I mean," Androulla says, rolling her eyes. "Not meeting Kostas."

Swapping her legs over, Olympia nods. "We talked about your relationship with Gary. My relationship with Gary. My impression of how you felt about visiting him, as a child."

There is a vibration from Androulla's bag. Pulling her phone out, she reads a message from Giannis.

'How's it going? Xxxxxxxxxxxxxxxxx', he has asked.

'Haven't gone in yet,' she replies, 'will call you after xxxxxxxxxxxxxxxxxx'.

Sliding her phone back, she looks to her mother. "And what did you say?" she asks.

The psychologist's door swings open.

"Androulla," Kostas summons her, with a sideways nod.

Androulla is halfway to lifting her bag before she thinks better of it. She will look more childlike with her arms hanging free, more in need of the parentage that Annita could grant her, officially. With a deep breath in, she enters the office.

"Have a seat," Annita instructs her.

It smells like pencil shavings and anti-bacterial spray. Closing the door, Androulla skirts past a low table of wooden blocks and plastic animals, her footsteps inaudible for the plush green carpet. She lowers herself into a chair across the desk from Annita. Books press inwards from the shelves on either side, while rain dribbles down a rectangular window. Androulla blinks, having forgotten the weather in the windowless hallway.

"One moment," Annita says, writing over the bottom line of a textbox. "I'm just finishing off . . ."

"That's okay." Androulla fiddles with the splayed end of one of her plaits.

With a final dot, Annita turns to a new page. "Shall we speak English?"

"Okay," Androulla says, lowering her hands.

With a lilting accent, Annita begins, "Full name, Androulla Dixon. Age, twenty-four years. And we're here to discuss your stepfather's application to adopt you?"

"Yes," Androulla confirms.

Annita marks something down on her clipboard. "I want to start by asking, in your opinion, what is the reason for this application? Why do you want your stepfather to adopt you?"

Androulla leans against the hard back of her chair. There are the practical reasons, the most prevalent being that she wants to remain in Cyprus. The English passport that she inherited from her father has been no use since Britain left the European Union. She did have a Greek one, until it expired amid her teenaged dissentions from her mother. Androulla could renew it, but in those years she drew closer to her stepfather and, by extension, to Cyprus. She came to think of Greece as snobbish, due to Olympia's constant tutting and correcting Kostas's 'village' Greek. Now, Androulla considers herself more Cypriot than Greek or English.

"Kostas has been in my life for as long as I can remember. He raised me. I'd like it to be true, when he introduces me as his daughter," Androulla says.

"So it's emotional," Annita surmises.

Androulla nods. "Yes."

Annita makes another note. "But you still have contact with your biological father, Gary Dixon. Correct?"

"I haven't seen him for two years. But we text occasionally," Androulla concedes.

Lowering her pen, Annita studies her. "And how is that relationship?"

Androulla grimaces. "He can be bullying."

"Towards you?"

"I don't think it's just me. It's the way he is," she says. "He says things that he knows will upset people, and he laughs."

"Can you give an example?" Annita probes.

Androulla's back feels as stiff as her chair's. She notices bite marks in one of several pencils in a stand, and wonders about the last words it wrote. "He used to make comments about how I looked. Like, I had really bad acne when I was younger. I know my skin's not great now," she adds, "but . . ."

Annita shakes her head, as though she cannot make out a blemish.

"I stayed in the house for days at a time because I was so self-conscious, I didn't want anyone to see me," Androulla says. "I remember I unwrapped a chocolate bar when I was feeling sad about it once, I must have been twelve or thirteen. And he said, 'So what, you're just going to be a big fat spotty thing, are you'. He called me 'pig' when he caught me making toast. And still now, I find it hard . . ."

Staring downwards, she feels Annita's eyes travel across her narrow shoulders. The scratching of her pen comes as a relief.

"You say you feel that Kostas raised you. What does that mean?" Annita asks.

"He was there," Androulla says, looking up. "Not just on weekends or holidays. He put me to bed every night when *Mamá* was studying. He calmed me down every morning when I wanted to stay home from nursery. He took time off work when I was sick, and when I had school assemblies."

"But how do you define that closeness? I mean," Annita says, searching the ceiling, "why do you feel that he is more like a father than a stepfather to you?"

"Because we argue," Androulla says. At the stricken look upon the psychologist's face, she explains, "We fall out with each other the way that only a parent and child can. I have a stepmother too, so I know the difference. With her, I have to be almost . . . polite? Like she's an aunt or something. I've never felt that with Kostas."

As Androulla talks, Annita's eyes grow brighter. Her notes are spilling over the ends of her textboxes by the time they conclude.

"I think that's everything I want to ask you," she says, turning her page back and forth. "As I told your parents, I'll submit my assessment before your case goes to court. There may be a home inspection first. You live with your parents, *nai*?"

"Yes," Androulla lies, as instructed. Her ring finger feels light upon her lap.

"Perfect," Annita says. "I'll walk you out."

Neither Androulla nor her parents breathe a word until they have ridden the lift down from the courthouse and crossed the road, their heads bowed to the rain.

"We did it!" Olympia cheers, when they reach their car.

An old Ford Focus, streaked with dust.

"I think that went well, didn't it?" Androulla says, climbing into the backseat.

"Really well," her mother agrees. "Don't you think, Kosta?"

Kostas is last to pull his door shut. Despite the grey sky, he takes his sunglasses from the glove compartment and shields his eyes. "The psychologist seems to think it's a straightforward case," he says.

"So what's wrong?" Androulla asks, as she digs through her bag for her phone.

A leaf from an orange tree lands on the windscreen, sodden.

"I don't know," Kostas says, bowing his head. "I feel kind of bad for Gary."

Olympia's shoulders rise.

"Why?" Androulla asks, drawing her phone out in a tight grip. "He did this to himself."

"Yeah. I guess so," Kostas says.

A raindrop hits the orange leaf, making it twitch, before he starts the car. As it rumbles to life, Androulla catches sight of her face in the wing mirror, bare of makeup and framed by plaits. She put on her most shapeless floral dress this morning, to convey her innocence, mere moments after her husband had bent her over their bathroom sink.

THE TENTH

ANDROULLA FACES THE BATHROOM mirror. The bulb above it casts a jaundiced light. She inspects her arms in her sleeveless dress, holding them away from her sides and tracing the lines of her triceps down. She is pinching at her flesh again when Giannis pokes his head around the door.

"Red," he says, with his eyes on her low neckline.

Androulla looks down at the garment, clinging from her shoulders to her calves. "Yeah," she says, slowly.

They share a laugh.

"You're ready early." Giannis takes his toothbrush from a bleary glass, rattling Androulla's, and runs it under the tap.

"We're going in, like, fifteen minutes," she says.

"What?"

Their eyes meet in the mirror.

"It starts at seven," Androulla reminds him.

The tap squeaks off under Giannis's palm.

"Shit," he says, driving his toothbrush into his mouth.

While he brushes, Androulla cranes to see to her lipstick, then squeezes out of the bathroom and into a leather jacket.

There is a chill in the air outside their apartment building. Blue light shoots through the dusky sky from the headquarters of Wargaming Limited. Like moths, they move towards it, Androulla with her hand curled around Giannis's arm.

Beyond the Wargaming tower, they enter the 'old' side of their neighbourhood, the settlement that existed before a capital city sprung up around it. The streetlights dim and grow sparser. The pavements trail off as if half-forgotten. Every house is either caving in with broken shutters, or neatly kept behind ornate window guards.

"It's humid," Giannis says.

"I heard it might rain," Androulla admits.

At the sound of a car approaching, Giannis falls into single file behind her. Its headlights illuminate the sign above a set of turquoise double doors.

Androulla stops, tripping her husband on her heels. "Sorry . . . This is it."

The doors rasp open. Creeping inside, Androulla inhales candle smoke and blinks to adjust to the golden light. She isn't inside, she sees, but under a shelf of ceiling that precedes a courtyard. Plastic wine glasses line a white-clothed table to her left. To her right, leaflets stud a noticeboard, advertising one-man shows and acoustic guitar concerts. One of them flinches under Giannis's forefinger.

"Do we just walk in? I don't know," Androulla murmurs.

"I told you we were early," Giannis says, as their footsteps echo across the courtyard.

Androulla runs her hand over a smooth arched wall. She turns her face up to the moon, shining through a veil of cloud.

"Wow," Giannis says, stopping beside her.

Their fingers lace together and a fresh smell threatens rain.

A voice sounds overhead. With her neck aching, Androulla brings her gaze down to a metal staircase on the far wall. They follow the commotion up onto a roof terrace, where a cloth screen hangs above a makeshift stage. Black folding chairs are set up as though for a wedding ceremony. In the aisle between them, a boy is leaning over a projector.

"Welcome," calls a woman, with dark roots showing through her blonde curls. "Have a seat. We'll begin shortly."

"Thank you." Androulla surveys the chairs, four on each side and none of them taken past the first two rows. "Where do you want to sit?" she asks her husband.

He points to a middle row. "Is here okay?"

"Sure."

Androulla lets out a sigh as she sinks down, relieved to have the buffer of several rows between herself and the stage. She hasn't attended many events like this since she left London. It was in the Southbank Centre that she had first met Giannis, at the reading of a British-born Cypriot poet named Leonidas Argyrou. Androulla had jumped to secure tickets, admiring Argyrou's work. She had sat at the front, anticipating his entrance, until visibly Cypriot cliques appeared. With a sideways look at her companion, Androulla shrank into herself. Naomi was four years her junior, with mousy hair and ruddy skin that betrayed her Englishness at a glance. She might respect the poet's work, but she wouldn't appreciate its deconstruction of post-colonial Cyprus, Androulla realised, let alone understand its take on the complexities of growing up Cypriot in Britain. How could she? How could Androulla have brought her to sit among people who had lived that struggle?

"Is this seat taken?" a voice sounded, over her shoulder.

With her cheeks burning, Androulla turned. A boy in a pale sweatshirt and jeans was standing over her. He sounded Australian, and yet he bore the same copper skin and coarse hair as most of the audience.

"No," she said.

The chair squeaked as he sat down beside her.

"Thanks."

Smiling, wordlessly, Androulla looked to Naomi. The girl was hunched over her phone, jabbing a message to her latest boyfriend.

Androulla stifled a sigh. She turned back to her new neighbour and caught a forest-like scent. "Are you here on your own?" she asked.

He shot her a rueful smile. "Bit of a sad case, aren't I? I just happened to be visiting London and I saw that this guy was in town," he said, gesturing to the empty stage. "He's a real inspiration of mine."

"Mine too," Androulla said, feeling her eyes turn bright.

"You write poetry?" the boy asked.

"Fiction," she answered, before remembering herself with a blush. "Not seriously, just in my spare time. How about you?"

"I'm a poet, yeah. Also in my spare time," the boy grinned. He extended his hand. "I'm Giannis."

"Androulla," she said, taking it.

A cough came from behind her.

"Oh," she said, sitting back. "And this is Naomi, my . . . friend."

"Hey," Giannis said, leaning over her.

The screen before them lights up, the name of the event running off it at a diagonal. As her assistant scuttles backwards, the blonde-haired woman takes charge of the projector. Pulling her jacket in, Androulla follows the breeze over her shoulder. She takes in the one and two-storey houses topped with water tanks, the yellowed apartment buildings and the glass high-rises that dwarf even them, towards the centre. To walk from the oldest part of Nicosia to the newest, spanning so much history, takes under twenty minutes. It is amazing that so much time can be folded into so little, Androulla thinks.

Giannis squeezes her hand, pressing her rings into her finger. Wincing, she faces the stage. The screen is fixed, the blonde-haired woman introducing herself as Sara. She is a member of this pan-European platform, she explains in English, hosting events around the continent to promote young poets at home and abroad. One such poet has come with her from

Sweden. Another has flown in from Germany. There are two from Cyprus, one Greek-speaking and one Turkish.

Androulla looks around. Thankfully, no one in the audience appears ruffled by the revelation that one of tonight's performers has crossed the border from the north. There aren't many people to ruffle – two older couples, a family with slouching teenagers, and those at the front who must know the poets somehow – for most of the seats remain empty. Looking back, Androulla can't believe she met Giannis that day at the Southbank Centre. There were so many bodies inside and outside the building that she spent the evening twisting sideways, throwing out 'sorry's every which way. That's what the people there wanted her to think, Leonidas Argyrou would have said, that she was taking up space. Here, there is space enough that Androulla could leap around windmilling her arms if she wanted to, and call it art, call it protest, call it a one-woman show. No one would stop her, but few people would reserve even free tickets.

"Without further ado," Sara says, extending her hand. "Let's hear from our first poet."

They clap the German woman onto the stage. She has short-cropped grey hair, is dressed as though for a country walk and reads three poems from the lectern. While their Greek and English translations are projected onto the screen behind her, they do no justice to the hissing and popping sounds that she clearly builds her work around. It is more soundscape than soul-bearing, not to Androulla's taste, though she admires the woman's energy.

After her, the Swedish poet takes the stage. He looks to be in his late twenties and hard-up, possibly for effect. His poems are short and end with dark punch lines. He recites them without pause in a billowing monotone, his eyes fixed to the horizon as if he means to conjure a spirit. Androulla cannot focus for her husband's trembling shoulders. Before she can nudge him, others laugh and the poet looks relieved.

"Thank you," he says, as he exits the stage.

"That was brilliant," Giannis says, wiping a finger across his eye.

Androulla smiles. She watches the screen, unmoved, until the next poet's work appears. '*Évreche símera*', it is titled. 'It Rained Today', by Pantelis Efstathiou.

Pantelis shuffles across the stage. Despite his full beard and belly, the darting of his round eyes tells Androulla that he is not much older than she is. He half-drops his page to the lectern, rumpling it. He wipes his hands down his sides, looks up. Their eyes meet. Androulla draws in a breath, newly aware of the darkness.

Casting his gaze over the rest of the audience, Pantelis begins. "'*Évreche símera . . .*'"

Androulla squeezes Giannis's hand. '*She*', the poet pronounces it. *Évre-'she'*, the Cypriot way, instead of the Greek *évre-'he'*. Giannis squeezes back. Androulla has told him the story, about a childhood visit to her great grandfather on Kostas's

27

side. It was raining. *Vréhe*, Androulla said, the way that her mother had taught her. Her great grandfather, who came from a village high in the Troodos Mountains, tutted and ribbed her. Who did she think she was talking to, the Queen of England? *Vréhe*, he mimicked, affectionately. This was Androulla's nickname until she replaced her Greek with the Cypriot Dialect, much to her mother's dismay. Shortly afterwards, her great grandfather died.

"'*Évreche símera*'," Pantelis repeats, at the start of his second stanza.

The breeze picks up and he catches his page at the edge of the lectern, no longer faltering. Androulla sits up taller. These words would have carried less weight, coming from Leonidas Argyrou. It is always raining in England. In the year that Androulla has lived in Cyprus, there have been so few rainy days that she can recall every one of them, vividly. Even those that are uneventful feel significant.

"'*Évreche símera*'," Pantelis says, again.

His voice grows stronger as he reads. Turning his page, he drops his hands to his sides. His words feel truthful, searing. Androulla trails them across the screen until her vision blurs.

"Thank you," Pantelis concludes.

By the time she has blinked her eyes dry, he is gone. In his place stands the girl from the north, perfect in her fitted jumpsuit. She reads one poem in Turkish before switching to English, her accent not lisping like a Greek's or lilting like a Greek-Cypriot's, but jarred and persevering. Androulla looks at

Giannis. He is wearing a smirk of desire that she can feel mirrored upon her own face. She listens to the poet's musings on the Turkish invasion of nineteen-seventy-four without reading along. Despite her best efforts, Androulla's eyes remain fixed upon the girl at the lectern.

Something hits her nose and she turns her face upwards. The patter of applause gives way to rainfall, sending shrieks up from the audience.

"Oh, no!" Sara cries, coming across the stage. She points over her shoulder. "Panteli, this is your fault. It's because of your poem about the rain . . ."

With bowed heads, the group laughs.

"That was everyone, just in time," Sara says, shielding her eyes. "Please join us for a complimentary drink downstairs. There should be enough shelter for all of us . . ."

Gathering their belongings, they hurry back down to the entranceway. They huddle beneath the shelf of ceiling, tepid white wine glasses in hand, and smile. The thought of initiating a conversation makes Androulla grip her glass tight. It felt easier in London, when she was working as an administrator in an estate agent's and had to confront strangers, daily. Since moving to Cyprus, she has worked from home as a ghostwriter and forgotten her confidence, she fears.

"You should talk to him," Giannis says, when Pantelis rounds the corner.

"What?" Androulla says.

"You liked his stuff the best, didn't you?" Giannis says, jerking his head towards the poet. "You should tell him. He'd love to hear that."

"I don't know," Androulla starts.

As Pantelis stops to pour himself a drink, Giannis pushes her towards him. She stumbles and catches the poet's heel.

"I loved your work," she blurts out, by way of apology.

Pantelis turns, slowly, to face her in full. Androulla tucks her hair back, conscious of how close-pressed they are beneath the limited shelter.

"Oh. Thank you," he smiles, revealing uneven rows of tobacco-stained teeth. "I'm glad you enjoyed it."

His eyelashes are so thick that Androulla thinks she could count them. She nods. Voices pick up around them. Pantelis's smile slackens and he stretches it wider again.

"Can I find it anywhere? Online, or . . ?" Androulla gestures.

"I post on Instagram, sometimes," Pantelis says, taking out his phone.

He holds it, limply, while Androulla types his username into hers.

She smiles. "That's great, thanks. It was nice meeting you."

"And you," Pantelis says, bobbing his head. "*Kaló apógevma.*" He leaves the building in a trail of cigarette smoke.

Androulla turns to see her husband talking to the poet from the north. She finishes her wine, grimacing at its sourness, and places her glass back on the table. Then she feels Giannis's hand on her back.

"Ready?" he asks. "It looks like it's still raining, but . . ."

"That's okay. It's novel, isn't it?" Androulla says, pulling open the doors.

"Novel?" he repeats, pointing a second time at the poster for tonight's event. "Don't be silly, Wife. This was poetry."

"Ha, ha," she says, taking his arm.

They step out into the rain.

THE SEVENTEENTH

SITTING BACK FROM HER laptop, Androulla takes a sip of her coffee. Plain black, the way she always drinks it. 'Plain' was a word that she had thought was synonymous with 'black', before she moved to Cyprus. In England, no one sweetens anything unless you ask them to, and if there is no extra charge they make clear that they are going out of their way. Androulla ordered her first coffee in Cyprus without saying *skéto* and had to throw it away, mouth pinched. A waste, her mother tutted.

There has been less taking away since then. Androulla and Giannis have their rent and bills to pay. She works through most weekends, taking on extra jobs from the ghostwriters' platform that she is part of. He attends twice-weekly Hospitality, Tourism and Events Management classes at UCLan, and bartends for more than the twenty hours per week that he is supposed to, as a foreign student. Androulla frets about this, constantly. Giannis reminds her that he only signed up for his

Master's course as a means of staying in Cyprus. His great, great grandparents moved to Australia during the gold rush, and so he has no family here to sponsor him. If the police find that he is working illegally, he could be deported and barred from returning, Androulla argues. What then? If the police come sniffing around the bar, their questions won't be for Giannis, he assures her, but for his darker-skinned colleagues. And even with him working overtime, Androulla cannot deny that they are struggling.

Placing her coffee down, she leans over her laptop. It takes up a good portion of the round table that they have squeezed in among rickety chairs, a short grey sofa that was her grandparents', and two bookshelves. A television sits atop one of them, just above eye-level so their necks ache if they watch it for too long. This is rare. The woody scent of the books, stacked alongside and on top of each other, distracts Androulla. As the silence impends, she forces herself to keep writing. She clatters across her keyboard, something about a family recipe from times gone by and the cosy feeling it evokes. The number of cookbooks she works on would suggest that those who are skilled in the kitchen have no hope with a pen. They all follow a similar formula, with the chef's notes conceding that they learned one recipe after a holiday to Southern Italy or Spain – could Androulla come up with a more authentic backstory?

Her phone lights up. Despite having put it on silent, she answers it.

"Hey," Naomi greets her. "How are you?"

"I'm good," Androulla says, automatically. "How are you?"

"I literally just woke up," Naomi groans. "Last night . . ."

"Oh, god." Switching her phone to loudspeaker, Androulla watches their call time tick to thirteen, fourteen, fifteen seconds before the screen goes dark. It is five p.m. her time, meaning three p.m. in England. "What happened? Did you go out?" she asks.

Naomi sighs. "Basically," she says.

Recognising this as the beginning of a long story, Androulla saves her work and closes her laptop. She feels lightheaded as she stands up, possibly because of the strange grey light and the rain that has been falling on and off all day, she thinks. Or because she has yet to eat anything but almonds. With her coffee in hand, she takes her phone call into the kitchen. The light is inescapable for its boxy dimensions. The window that should offer a view of the Pentadaktylos Mountains shows only a mist beyond the city's high-rises. Androulla sets her phone down on the counter.

"So they came to ours for pre's," Naomi's voice echoes.

"Wait, who did?" Androulla asks.

Naomi names five people that Androulla has never met, and yet whose lives she knows, intimately. She and Naomi speak most days. Sometimes, Naomi has more to report. Like when she failed her first year at Portsmouth after too much time spent partying, and had to retake it. Her parents think she is doing a Master's Degree this year, rather than finishing her Bachelor's in Childhood and Youth Studies with Psychology. When her life is less eventful, she tells Androulla which of her housemates are or are not sleeping together, and what she and the others think about it. Androulla can laugh about this in a way that she struggles to when it comes to Naomi's own escapades. Already, Androulla understands that twenty-one is much younger than it feels. However old they get, no matter what people say in favour of nature over nurture, Naomi will always be her little sister.

As Naomi recounts a night of drunken abandon, Androulla prizes open the fridge. She drags a silver bowl from the lowest shelf and lifts it onto the counter with both hands.

"Yeah," she exhales, uncovering it.

"Which no one understands," Naomi is saying. "They broke up a year ago."

"That is a long time," Androulla agrees.

An earthy smell rises. Spooning her black-eyed beans from the water they have been soaking in to a pot on the hob, she cuts into a courgette.

"Everyone was out of it by the time we got there, it was a mess. Anyway," Naomi says. "Long story short, me and Tommy . . ."

The knife slips in Androulla's hand, almost taking her thumb off. She lets out a sharp breath. A cackle sounds from the countertop.

"I thought you were doing something with Stan," she protests, turning the courgette upright on her chopping board.

"I was," Naomi says, "last week."

Hearing the grin in her voice, Androulla sighs.

"You can't judge," Naomi retorts. "You're way worse than me, with the stuff you get up to."

"In the safety of my home, with my husband," Androulla reminds her, leaning close to her phone for emphasis.

"Yeah, now," Naomi says.

Androulla can do nothing but join her in laughing at this.

Naomi lets out a yawn. "What are you making, anyway?"

"*Louví*," Androulla says, pushing thick discs of courgette aside with the blunt edge of her knife.

They have been in each other's lives long enough that she doesn't have to translate the name of this dish, as she would for her other English friends. Their mothers met in a prenatal group when Olympia was pregnant with Androulla, and Naomi's mother was expecting her first child. Oscar. He and Androulla were inseparable in their early years. They were going to get married, they declared, to coos of delight from their parents. One day, Androulla showed Oscar a game she had discovered, a squirming pursuit of ecstasy that took place upon the arm of a sofa. Olympia marched her home in a tight grip when she found out.

Then Oscar's mother had Naomi, as though to ensure that he and Androulla would never be left alone again. Androulla was outraged. While their parents carried on downstairs, she scowled at the toddler. As an only child, she couldn't fathom the bonds that existed between brothers and sisters. She hated all her friends' siblings for dividing their attention. The older ones, she had to sit sullenly and tolerate. But Naomi was easy to shove out the way when no one was looking.

She was in Oscar's bedroom when he 'dared' Androulla to give him a handjob. It was the night before Androulla's thirteenth birthday, and she was staying the night on his floor. Even as Naomi asked what he meant and shrieked at the answer, Androulla felt a pulse between her legs. She sat very still on the futon while Oscar explained that this was a natural thing, though no one else should hear about it. Androulla made a reasonable show of hesitating before they pulled the blanket off Oscar's bed, and hid underneath it in case of intruders. In the airless fug, she stared at him. She was in awe of his form, having lacked a father or brothers. Her stepfather she had never seen naked below the waist. It wasn't appropriate, her mother had said.

"Do you want to try?" Androulla asked, conscious of her audience.

Naomi gave Oscar's penis a prod before squealing and retracting her forefinger. After that, it was up to Androulla. Oscar asked her to put it in her mouth, but she was afraid of getting pregnant. In the end, he sat bolt upright and clouded a glass of water. The next day, before they went to the cinema, he told Androulla that he might be gay.

It was homophobia that they blamed for his death, months later. Bullies at school. An unspoken lack of self-acceptance. Androulla went to his funeral with numb limbs and a pounding heart, terrified that she was at fault. When she saw Naomi, waiflike and practically infantile for so black a dress, her fears evaporated. She knew that Naomi, too, would do anything to take back what she had said that day, about how upset she would be if her brother never made her an aunty. After the service, Androulla drew her close.

"You're my sister now," she whispered, into Naomi's matted hair.

They were bound together then, all the scowling and shoving behind them. They shared stories and secrets and the same love lost. And yet, Androulla would never attempt to possess Naomi, wholly, as she had Oscar and other friends. She had seen that no one's life was within her control, no matter how well she thought she knew them. That any jealousy was futile.

"I miss Greek food," Naomi whines.

"Cypriot food," Androulla corrects her.

"Cypriot, sorry. That's what I meant."

Filling her pot with water, she pokes down the beans that float to the surface and returns to the sink. Over her shoulder, Naomi's voice is indistinct.

"Hang on, I'm just washing a lemon," Androulla calls.

It is one that she picked from a neighbour's tree, along with the oranges in her fridge. A citric scent rises from the skin, rough under Androulla's thumb, before she shakes it dry. Then, just as her grandmother taught her, she squeezes the juice of one half into the pot and throws its skin in after.

"What were you saying?"

"I want to come and see you," Naomi says.

"Come," Androulla bids her, setting the pot to boil.

"I can't yet, I've got my dissertation to finish."

"Mmn. Giannis's is due soon as well," Androulla says.

"Have you guys figured out what you're going to do after that?" Naomi asks. "His visa's running out soon, isn't it?"

"He has until August," Androulla says, as froth the colour of bile foams up in her pot. Turning the heat down, she spoons it out into the sink. "He's started looking at other courses, to get ahead. The process took ages last time."

"Is he literally just going to keep getting degrees until he's been there long enough to apply for residency?" Naomi asks, with a hint of amusement.

Grimacing, Androulla bends to take out two dishes. "I mean, yes. But normally that process would take seven years. My parents have spoken to a lawyer who thinks I can get naturalised within five, now that Kostas has adopted me. And then Giannis will be able to stay here through marriage."

"Once you're actually married," Naomi says.

The dishes hit the countertop with twin thuds.

"Yes," Androulla concedes.

She eyes a chip in the porcelain. Sometimes, she regrets telling even her closest confidante that she and Giannis have yet to sign the papers. They can go weeks at a time, giggling and calling each other Wife, before she remembers that days before they were due to exchange vows, it came to light that her status in Cyprus was under threat. She couldn't claim to be a dependant on her parents if she was married. She could have renewed her Greek passport, and remained with her husband on the grounds that she was a citizen of the European Union. But then the court wouldn't have rushed her adoption case through, convinced that she was on the brink of being sent back to England with nowhere to live, and she wouldn't be on the fast-track to getting her Cypriot citizenship. She loves Giannis. She hates that his path into Cyprus isn't straightforward. But she has dreamed of being recognised as Cypriot – socially, legally – for years longer than she has known him. When she comes close to caving, she recalls her great grandfather chanting *vréhe* and her mother tutting at his accent, and she holds her ground. She and Giannis couldn't cancel their wedding, with so many friends and family members packed to fly in from England and Australia. And so they staged a celebrant ceremony.

"That's a lot of debt to take on in the meantime," Naomi says, warily.

Through the boiling water, Androulla stares at the beans that cost her two euros per kilo, dried. That feeds her and Giannis for almost a week, with slightly varying combinations of vegetables each night.

"It is," she says. "But Cyprus means a lot to him too. He's tried applying for jobs here, but companies can't hire third-country nationals unless they can prove that there are no qualified candidates in the EU. So a student visa is his only option, really."

"And are you okay to keep claiming you're a dependant on your parents?" Naomi asks.

"Should be," Androulla says, spooning more froth out of her pot.

"What would happen if they left, though? Like, if they suddenly decided to move back to London," Naomi says.

Androulla leans her spoon back against the pot with a 'clink'. "That'll never happen, Brexit felt like way too big a rejection for them. They're happier here."

"Don't let them tell my mum that," Naomi says.

"When do you want to come out, anyway?" Androulla asks her.

Silencing the timer on her phone, she strains the beans from their darkened water. Flecks of it burn her wrist and she winces.

"I was thinking in the summer?" Naomi's voice sounds, behind her. "I need some time to just lie on the beach after this year, honestly."

Androulla tips the beans into a pot of fresh water, affecting a jovial tone. But she means it when she says, "This isn't going to be like a trip with your housemates, you know. You're getting a wellness retreat with me. To detox."

"I need it," Naomi admits, through a laugh.

Almost as soon as Androulla has tipped the courgette and the second half of lemon into her pot, there is the sound of boiling. She turns, frowning. The water is still. It is the window at which rain is pattering, yet again. She squints against its grey light and raises a hand to her head.

"August?" Naomi suggests.

"Sounds good," Androulla says, just as Giannis comes through the front door. Giving him a wave, she sets another fifteen minute timer on her phone. "I mean it about the detox, though. No drinking, no smoking, no boys," she adds.

Naomi hangs up, laughing.

"Okay, Mum," Giannis says, dropping his keys onto the counter.

Androulla is smiling, going to kiss him, when she hears this word. Mum. It rings out, discordantly, and she slides from her husband's embrace.

The Twenty-Eighth

ANDROULLA LOOKS SUITABLY THIN in her white shirt and the pleated skirt that falls over her knees, as close to prepubescent as she can at twenty-four. She has been taking her acne pills for almost a month, and still has an unfortunate number of spots. But the skin around them looks brighter. Her pores have shrunk, the redness calmed from her cheeks and jawline. She doesn't balk at her reflection in the bathroom mirror. Instead of plaiting her hair, she smooths it back with a polka dot headband. Another girlish look.

"Cute," Giannis murmurs, as she leaves him to sleep off his hangover from a night at work.

She washes the morning-after taste of him from her mouth and spits it out with her toothpaste.

In the car, her parents say nothing. Their seats shrivel inwards as rain drums down upon the roof. Androulla opens her window a fraction, to let some air in, and her stepfather cranes around to give her a warning look. She takes a deep breath of the petrichor and closes it. The windscreen wipers groan from side to side on too slow a setting, as if Kostas is in denial of the blinding volume of water that is building up between their movements. When they stop in traffic, he sighs. Androulla's stomach grumbles.

"Have you eaten breakfast?" her mother asks.

"Yeah," she lies.

They park on the side road opposite the courthouse. A man strides by with an umbrella in hand, ruffling the leaves of the orange trees that line the pavement. Androulla feels lightheaded.

"Ready?" her stepfather asks.

An old Mazda trundles past and they vault from their seats, slamming their doors shut and making a break for the crossing. Androulla holds her hands up to protect the makeup that she has applied. Nude eye-shadow with no liner. Highlighter and no bronzer. A motorbike tears towards a deepening puddle and she stumbles back from its spray.

"Go," Kostas commands, when the green man appears.

Grigoris, people call this symbol. Like he is someone they know personally, unlike the abstract figure that oversees the crossings in England. As the rain falls harder, Androulla forgets her embarrassment in front of the halted cars and picks her pace up to a jog. Her parents speed ahead of her, sending water up from their heels. Androulla curses herself and them both for getting so used to the rain in England that they stopped bothering with umbrellas. Her Cypriot grandmother keeps two in the boot of her car at all times, though she can't have use for them more than a few days each year.

Inside the courthouse, they stop. Panting, Androulla pushes her headband back and asks if her makeup looks okay. Her mother leans to inspect it, her jasmine scent made sharper by the rain. Androulla fights her urge to step backwards.

"Is that really what we're worried about, girls?" Kostas asks, walking around a steel arm that looks like it should beckon the lift.

"It's locked," Androulla reminds him. "We need someone who works here."

In the corner of her eye, she watches him persist with his search for a button.

"You're fine," her mother says, at last.

As Androulla steps away from her, the doors behind them part.

"*Kaliméra sas*," Kostas says, straightening to greet the man who walks in.

Smoothing his hair dry, the man smiles. He is clean-shaven and wearing a suit. When Kostas explains that they are due in court at nine a.m., the man summons the lift with a small silver key. As they ride up, he tells them that he works with their lawyer, Mary. She is excellent.

"Good to know," Kostas says, with one of his nervous laughs.

Androulla grits her teeth. The lift reaches the height of its grubby glass shaft and drops an inch before the doors open.

Their lawyer is waiting in a grey-tiled corridor. "Mary," she introduces herself, shaking their hands in turn.

Androulla studies her fading hair, the small face behind her glasses, and wonders how someone so short and kindly-looking can be convincing in a courtroom. She feels her stomach sinking, but Kostas greets the lawyer with a bolder smile than he has worn all morning.

Mary leads them to a high desk, across which they must slide their passports. Kostas asks Androulla for hers in 'cleaner' Greek than he ever speaks, and her mother gives her an assured smile. Then they wait. Despite the rain, the view beyond the floor-to-ceiling windows is breathtaking. It displays more of the Kyrenia Mountain range than Androulla can see from her home, its peaks dotted with verdant shrubs from the winter rainfall. Soon the summer will come, and the landscape will dry to a barren brown.

This is hard to believe today, but it is as inevitable a fate as Androulla writes for the girls in her stories. She feels like one of them in her formless attire, staring at the Turkish flag that is embossed on the mountainside and wondering how north and south became so divided. In reality, she understands the history and the politics. She reads the articles on both sides of the reunification debate with a raised brow. But her escapism from the Cyprus Problem – from all her problems, in fact – is inventing characters that tilt their heads and blink at the world, bemused by its harshness. Girls whose comfortable shoes she can step into for an hour each evening, to see what it would feel like never to have been corrupted. Not politically, not personally. What it would feel like to be shocked by invasions of land and flesh, rather than scarred by them. For Androulla, that is more pornographic than any of the videos she watches later, when Giannis is out at the bar. That innocence, that luxury of seeing the world through wide eyes, is her fantasy. The low-stakes lives that she creates for her fictional selves are far further flung than any scenes of rough or wild sex. But they won't thrill anyone else enough to publish, and so she will stay stuck writing undergraduates' essays and cookbook content for a living.

"*Oriste*," the man behind the counter says, sliding her passport back.

At the sight of its newly black cover, Androulla feels her lip curl.

She and her parents follow Mary past desks of lawyers, stacking files and scanning documents, into the courtroom. It isn't what she was expecting. A corner office, not very large, with the same glass walls offering an extended view of the Kyrenia Mountains. Mary points Androulla and her parents to a back bench before taking a seat at the front. Her reassurances echo through the empty space. There is a smell like varnish coming from nowhere that Androulla can pinpoint, and a closeness to the air. She takes shallow breaths until the door opens again, emitting Annita.

"Hello," the psychologist mouths, her long hair overhanging the folder that she is clutching to her chest. She gives a smile, too curt to be consoling, and sets herself up alongside Mary.

Androulla crosses and uncrosses her legs. Her mother maintains a neutral expression. Her stepfather stands, looks out the window, and resumes his seat.

A door bangs open against the far wall, the only one that is wood-panelled and not glass. Both of Androulla's parents stand now, her mother jogging her to do the same as a grey-bearded man takes his place on the bench above them. He looks like a Holy Week priest in his black gown, about to sing the Divine Liturgy from his altar. Once several other dark-clothed figures have filed in and taken their places beneath him, the Judge motions for them to be seated. Again, Androulla is last to react. The hardness of the bench resounds through her body, deafening her to his opening comments. His eyes flick upwards. It is only when her mother nudges her again that Androulla registers her name and nods, dumbly.

"*Kyría* Olympia Demetriou?"

Her mother raises a hand.

"*Kai o Kýrios* Kostas Demetriou?"

"*Naí,*" Kostas says.

With their presences confirmed, the Judge hands over to Mary, then to Annita. Both women stand to give their statements. Androulla fights to focus on what they are saying, but her heart keeps dropping like the lift before its doors opened, and the sensation prevents her from catching a word. She watches the rain hitting the window and wonders if it is making a sound, whether her ears are failing or the glass is succeeding.

The Judge is professing something. Androulla can see his mouth moving, can hear the droning of his voice. Her mother is tugging her upwards again. The Judge is raising his gavel. This isn't real, Androulla thinks. It is like a scene from fiction, simultaneously too outlandish and too clichéd for any that she would write. Nonetheless, the gavel comes down with a thud. Androulla blinks. The Judge is turning away, his witnesses gathering their papers.

"Is that it?" Androulla whispers.

Her stepfather doesn't answer the first time, and gives a discreet shrug the second. Mary leads them from the courtroom, stopping so that they can sign out with the man who took their passports.

"That was, like, less than ten minutes," Androulla says, to her mother.

"Let's see," Olympia murmurs.

As her stepfather leans over the counter, Androulla digs her fingernails into her palms. How can none of them understand what has just happened, whether or not their ordeal is over?

Mary turns her key for the lift. It isn't until they are sealed inside that she smiles, and says to Kostas, "*Na sas zísi.*" 'May she live you', as if Androulla is a new-born child.

Androulla's fists fall open. Her mother's eyes are full, her stepfather's laughter unrestrained as they gush their thanks. Despite the rain still running down it, the sky outside the lift shaft looks brighter. Androulla's adoption is complete.

"We're indebted to you," Kostas says.

He touches Mary's arm with the tenderness he might have touched a midwife's, if Olympia hadn't lost the only child he was able to give her, twenty years ago.

"You're a nice family," Mary says, shaking her head. "It's easy to see. That's why this case went through so fast."

The lift jerks to a halt. They revel in their success a few moments longer before stepping out into the rain. As Mary clacks away in her kitten heels, Androulla's parents squeal and chatter. Androulla lets them pull ahead, not bothering to shield her eyes from her running mascara, or to fold her arms across her translucent-turned shirt. She slumps in the back of the car, watches the courthouse drag by her window. And she thinks, with what the doctor has told her, that she may not be done with the adoption process yet. Not if she changes her mind about wanting a child.

APRIL

THE FOURTH

Leaving Giannis asleep, Androulla pulls on her raincoat and sets out from their apartment building. Stray cats scatter from the entrance where they must have been sheltering, one of them stopping mid-stride to stare at her, accusingly, as its fur goes flat to its head. Androulla murmurs an apology. The rain isn't hard but steady, pattering down upon her hood and making the pink bauhinia flowers droop along the pavements. She keeps her head bowed until she has to cross a road, then overacts her looks right-to-left for fear that her hood might obscure the sound of an approaching car.

She pushes it back when she enters the pharmacy, two streets over. The doors slide shut behind her, and she feels like a source of humidity in the cramped space. Unzipping her coat halfway, she fans the air into her collar.

"*Kaliméra*," calls the shop's owner, a portly man with grave eyes.

"*Geiá sas*," Androulla smiles.

Two girls look up from behind the counter. It was the taller, thinner one with the perfect makeup who served Androulla last month, when she came in for her first box of acne pills. Androulla hasn't forgotten the girl's way of pinching things between her acrylic nails, or the smell of her up close like coconuts. Recalling her embarrassment, she sniffs. From here, the smell of sun cream is undercut by something clinical. There is a herbal scent, too, that she cannot quite place.

As she browses the shelves, the other girl approaches her. This one is Androulla's height, fuller around the hips and chest with curly brown hair and a heinous jumper.

"Would you like some help?" she asks.

Androulla steps backwards and the girl comes with her.

"I was just looking for these pills," she starts.

"Which?" the girl proceeds, in a loud voice.

She has taken a pink box of them to the counter before Androulla can weigh it in her palm, see the price stuck on the side and change her mind. She was caught off guard last month, when she came in with the doctor's signed and stamped note to find that it was less prescription than recommendation. Because these pills are, in his words, 'one-hundred percent natural, no chemicals', their cost cannot be subsidised by any health organisation. When the tall girl explained this, it was Androulla's awkwardness that drove her to buy them anyway. She didn't actually believe they would work, having tried every other supplement, cream and dietary change to no avail. And yet here she is, calculating the number of extra words that she will have to write this month to cover the cost, as she fumbles for her bankcard.

"*Efcharistó*," the curly-haired girl says, slipping the box into a bag.

Her colleagues echo her thanks as Androulla turns from the counter. She is bowing her head before she has stepped out into the rain, with a feeling like she has stolen something. These pills are worth the stretch, she tells herself, even as the bag hangs weightlessly from her fingertips. After just four weeks of taking them, she feels better about her appearance, and that, actually, is priceless. She remembers what it was like to despise and bully her reflection as a teenager, how frustrating it was to hear of the unblemished girls at her school playing 'hard to get' or making their boyfriends wait for sex. Androulla would have slept with anyone, she thought, some nights, lying on her back with an insatiable hunger keeping her awake. If only she was even thinner. If only her skin was clear enough that her peers could see through it, to the willing girl that lay in wait underneath. If only the first boy she ever touched hadn't declared his disinterest and swiftly died, then Androulla might not have this coursing desire to prove herself, always followed by the comedown to mortal dread. It wasn't until after school that she garnered more attention, and still she craves it.

The smell of coffee greets her at home. Giannis is sitting at the table with his laptop, sipping from an *Orlando* mug.

"Hey. Where have you been?" he asks, standing to kiss her.

"Mmn. Not ready yet," Androulla says, turning her face.

Giannis plants his lips on her cheek. "But you've been out already," he protests.

"I didn't get close to anyone," Androulla says, shielding her mouth to stop any morning breath from escaping, "although that girl at the pharmacy tried her best."

Giannis's eyes turn bright. "The good-looking one?"

Passing her bag from one hand to the other, Androulla twists out of her raincoat. "The short one," she says, "with the curly hair. Doesn't wear any makeup."

"She does that to you as well?" Giannis says, slouching. "I thought I was special."

"You think she's the good-looking one, really?" Androulla asks, stepping into the kitchen.

"What are you doing? I'll make your coffee, go and sit down," Giannis murmurs, in an aside from their debate. Then he shrugs. "Yeah. The other one's a bit much for me, with the nails and stuff."

Androulla leans her weight back onto one heel. "That's actually really nice," she says.

Squeezing past her, Giannis pops open the kettle. "What do you mean?"

"I just think she's the less obvious choice. Most people would probably walk in there and look at the other girl," Androulla says, raising her voice over the running tap.

Giannis turns it off and sets the kettle to boil. "Like you do, you mean?" he grins.

Androulla hesitates only briefly before conceding a laugh. The noise of the kettle arcs up to a simmering 'click'.

"It's all unacceptable really, isn't it?" Giannis says, as he stirs her instant coffee.

He drops the teaspoon, clattering, into the sink and leads Androulla to the table.

"So, I've been looking at courses. For next year," he adds.

She goes on staring until he drops his gaze to the screen between them.

"There aren't a lot options relevant to what I've done before," he says, slowly. "I've got my BA in Hospitality and Tourism Management from Edith Cowan. MA in Hospitality, Tourism and Events Management from UCLan. Now, the thing to do to get me the longest stay here, would be a PhD."

Androulla takes a sip of coffee, burning her tongue. Even as she puts her mug down and stares into its steaming depths, she can feel Giannis watching her.

"I know you think it's a lot of debt to take on for a sector I could have just worked in," he says.

Androulla acknowledges this with a shrug of her eyebrows.

"But when I go to work, you're not happy either."

"Because it's illegal, the amount of overtime you do," she says, looking up at him.

"We need the money. And I like my job, I never wanted to be a student this long. I only got the first degree to piss about, like everyone else," Giannis says. With a worn sigh, he adds, "Obviously, if I could go back in time and choose to have done it here, I would. I'd be over halfway to naturalisation by now, and we wouldn't be having this conversation . . ."

"We also might not have met," Androulla says, to shock the monotone from his voice.

Giannis sits back. "That's true," he admits.

The rain drums on beyond the window.

"Can I be honest with you?" Giannis says, lifting his mug up in front of his chest. "When it comes to these conversations, I feel like you blame me for making our lives difficult. It's like you forget that this whole ordeal with Immigration is hard for me too, when I'm the one who's in danger of being deported. And I'm the one who's getting into debt, ultimately, not you." Halfway to drinking more coffee, he stops. "Do you think it doesn't hurt that I'm only allowed three months here as a tourist? My entire family is from here, even if they left generations ago. It's in my blood."

"I know that," Androulla says, in a warning tone.

"But you still think it's my fault for not coming here straight away, don't you? Or for not studying something more specialised," Giannis urges her.

She lets out a careful breath. "Look. This country has suffered colonisation, civil unrest, a coup and an invasion, in the last hundred years alone. There are diaspora around the world who are desperate to come home and can't, because there are no opportunities for them here. Or because their family left one too many generations ago, and so they can't claim citizenship. It's complicated."

"Not for you," Giannis says, quietly.

Androulla tenses at the accusation in his voice, the half-sentence left unspoken – that she is not even really from here – as if her own insecurity isn't enough to contend with. Perhaps worse still is the implication that she could simplify things for Giannis, if she just renewed her Greek passport instead of holding out for a Cypriot one. If she just gave up on the validation she has wanted and awaited, that has been integral to her identity, since she was a child.

Forcing her arm across the table, she opens her palm. "So many elements of this are shit, for both of us. I'm glad you enjoy your job. If anything, I'm jealous. I'd love to get out and meet people the way you have, but I'm not meant to be working at all as a 'dependant'. As much as I'm underpaid and I get lonely sometimes, I'm lucky to have a remote job that I can keep quiet. I can't quit," she says.

"I know," Giannis sighs, taking her hand.

Androulla squeezes his. "We will get there," she says. "I think we just have to be a bit patient with each other, and . . . everything."

Giannis nods.

"So, a PhD?" Androulla says, affecting a brighter tone.

"Yeah. I'm thinking at UNic," Giannis says, closing the lid of his laptop and looking off to one side. "What did you go out for, anyway?"

Androulla follows his gaze to her pharmacy bag. "Oh. Just some more of those pills for my skin," she says, brushing back an invisible strand of her hair.

With a click of his tongue, Giannis says, "And you gave that girl a taste of your morning breath . . ."

"You should have been there," Androulla teases, relieved to fall back on this lighter conversation, one that they can both see as plain fun for its ridiculousness.

Giannis laughs. "I do actually think she has a crush on me."

"Really? What are you even going in there for?" Androulla asks, lifting her coffee.

"Condoms," he says. "Or I was. Haven't been back for a while, obviously. Maybe I should pay her a visit."

"She probably thinks you've lost your touch." Androulla's laughter echoes into her mug.

"You can vouch for me there, then," Giannis says, with bright eyes.

Androulla sits back. For a moment, she sees her husband as she did over their first drink together. As a boy, who still took flights to see the world and not because he was under duress. Who loved poetry enough to attend a reading in a foreign city, alone and unabashed. Who she was so magnetically drawn to that she introduced Naomi as her friend and not her sister, to assure him of her connection to Cyprus. They talked about the island all night, what it was like to grow up both with and without it, and what they each thought of the British-born Cypriot poet's take on this. They gazed at each other – just like this –

for the remainder of Giannis's stay in London, sharing stories, jokes and book recommendations. The sex was unparalleled.

Later that summer, they met by chance in Cyprus. They knew then that it was love. A magnificent discovery, and a troubling one. It felt like having an unjust sentence passed, to realise that they couldn't stand the thought of not being together. Their relationship was an undertaking, with such a long and unaffordable distance for its members to cover, just to kiss each other. But it was fireworks, too. It was worth Giannis getting down on one knee with an emerald ring, to promise Androulla that one day, he wouldn't have to text her 'good morning'. He would roll over and say it to her face, with the breath and all.

They added an extra kiss to the ends of their messages for every month that they were apart before they moved to Cyprus, Giannis alone and Androulla with her politically disillusioned parents. The distance forced them to communicate well, but it was a strain. They had to keep the physical side of their relationship alive somehow, across all those hard borders. Perhaps that was what led them to talking so openly about who they found attractive outside of each other, what kind of porn they each watched and how much of it they could see themselves recreating, in real life.

Perhaps the familiarity of that, the flippancy of it, against the extraordinary hardship of everything else, is what leads Androulla to say, "I wouldn't mind."

"What?" Giannis asks.

She shrugs. "If it was just a physical thing, and there were no feelings involved. I actually think that could be kind of hot."

He lets a breath out through his teeth. "I am very lucky."

"You are," she says, intending to echo his light-hearted tone. But the words come out blunter, more forcefully than she means them to.

"Right." Shaking his head, Giannis stands to clear their coffee mugs. With *Orlando* in hand, he kisses her forehead. "Your skin does look good."

"Thanks."

Just a physical thing, Androulla thinks, as her husband makes for the kitchen. There is the crash of their mugs into the sink, then the sound of running water. She is conscious, with the rain dripping down the window and the cramps threatening her lower abdomen, that her period is about to come on. Two months of unprotected sex, and no sign of any trouble. Perhaps it truly is just a physical act, one that will never translate into anything more meaningful, for her.

The Twenty-First

WITH SPEARMINT TOOTHPASTE CLAGGING her mouth, Androulla climbs into bed. She is home alone, Giannis out at the bar. It is funny, she thinks, that he saves his drinking for his workdays. He has told her what it is like on busy nights, when the staff – including his manager – lean over and say 'the fridge is broken', code that it is time to go around the back and do a shot. They get to drink every cocktail that they misassemble. One bartender claims to misremember far more beer orders than the others. With him on shift, it is always a big night. Giannis has come home at three a.m. and thrown up before now.

Rolling onto her back, Androulla stares up at the white plastic ceiling fan. In the summer, its motion creates a horizontal current of sound, unlike the rain coming down outside her window. She closes her eyes and pictures this. Winter a downward motion, summer hot and sending everything sliding sideways as though slicked with sweat on a polished surface. The rain turns to white noise in her ears as she reaches one hand for her phone and the other under her duvet. As the video plays, her breaths get shallower. Something inside her body stretches higher and she arches to meet it, her eyes fixed upon the screen and, finally, closing.

The lamplight is there waiting when she reopens her eyes. The self-loathing is instant, another downward current of energy drawing her lips and eyebrows with it. She had heard men talk about this comedown, but never experienced it herself until she watched porn for the first time. Giannis's idea, to help them cope with long-distance. Before that, Androulla had relied upon her imagination in these moments, and rolled out of bed with a lighter step afterwards. Is that how many men are watching porn, that their entire sex has deemed this flash of disgust a natural response to ecstasy? Is Androulla un-feminist for joining them in it? She finds it hard to believe that women in the industry are safe and fairly treated, even when they start off talking to camera about how excited they are to do a scene. She touches the tab closed as if it is hot and lands back on her previous page.

'Polycystic Ovary Syndrome', glares its heading.

According to the NHS website, one of the main features of this condition is excess androgen, or high levels of male hormones in the body. With a sigh, Androulla rereads the paragraph about the increased production and activity of testosterone that she definitely has. That she was first affected by at three or four years old, and that led to her mother marching her home from Oscar and Naomi's in that tight grip. Perhaps Androulla is not so much a bad or un-feminist woman as she is not a woman, she thinks. Her figure disagrees, despite the curves that she has done her best to starve from it. It is at war with itself, internally and externally, chemically and cosmetically. She feels stranded inside it, as if she has entered the buffer zone that separates south and north Cyprus and neither side will let her back in.

Her ringtone startles her. Androulla silences it, her eyes fixed to the name onscreen. The rain falls harder beyond the window.

"Hello?" she answers, unblinking.

"Hello. Andy?" comes the reply.

"Yeah, I'm here. Hi." Fearing that her breaths still sound uneven, she sits up against her headboard.

Her father clears his throat. "How are you?"

"Fine," she says, hollowly. "How about you?"

"Yeah. Not bad, thanks."

His voice sounds different to how she remembers, higher-pitched and less commanding. Then stopped. Androulla pinches the corner of her duvet. When the silence grows too much in her ear, she switches her phone onto loudspeaker. The audio times in just as her father is coming to the end of a sentence.

"Sorry," she says, cringing. "I think I lost you there."

He gives a deadened laugh.

"What did you say?"

"Nothing, really. I just asked you what you'd been up to."

"Like today, or . . ? Sorry," she realises, shaking her head. "I'm not sure how to answer that."

Her father sighs. "We haven't spoken for a while, have we. Why is that? Why haven't you called me?"

At least he joins her in laughing at this.

"Right," she says, when they stop.

"When was the last time?" Gary asks.

"Two years ago," Androulla says, "when I told you I was planning to move to Cyprus."

"God, was it?"

"Yes. You weren't very happy about that, were you?"

"About what? You moving to Cyprus?" he asks.

"Mmn."

"I don't think I had a problem with that. I wasn't sure about the bloke you were seeing."

Androulla feels her eyebrows arch and tries to keep her voice from rising after them. "You'd never met him. All you knew was that he was from Cyprus and that that's what we'd connected over. Anyway, we're married now. I assume you got your invite to our wedding."

"Andy, what was I supposed to do? You sent me that with three weeks' notice. Claire and I had already booked to go to–"

"I gave you three weeks' notice because I didn't want you to come," Androulla snaps. "I didn't think it would be right, given that you'd never taken an interest in my husband. He was the one who convinced me to send it."

"There you go, then. You didn't want me there and I didn't come. It's done now, so there's no point getting upset," her father says. "He spoke to me too, you know."

Androulla stares at her phone.

"Your husband. What's his name? Yan, Yannis?"

"Giannis," Androulla corrects him, in an accent heavy with spite.

"Giannese," her father pronounces, poorly. "He called and said how much he thought it would mean to you if I could be there."

"And what did you say?" Androulla holds her breath.

"I told him I'd try, but I didn't want him getting your hopes up. Claire and I had a trip booked with some friends, and we just couldn't let them down in the end. They've got young kids, and it's almost impossible for them to arrange any time away . . ."

"So you let me down instead. Your kid," Androulla says.

"I knew you'd say that. But Andy, we haven't spoken for two years," Gary protests. "You've just said you didn't want me at your wedding, and now you're calling yourself my kid. It's like, do you want me to be your dad or not?"

"Oh, you're offering now, are you?" she retorts.

He sighs. "Alright. Let's just calm down a minute, shall we?"

Androulla closes her eyes. "Claire never wanted kids. She put up with me every other weekend for as long as she had to, and now the two of you are happy living your free, childless life. I get that," she says, evenly.

"Claire may not have wanted kids of her own, but that doesn't mean she loved you any less. You've got that wrong," her father insists.

"Right." Agitated, Androulla stands and fingers the beaded cord that hangs down with her blind.

"He seems nice," her father says, eventually. "Yannis."

"Giannis," Androulla says, again. Then, "He is."

"Stupid accent, though," her father adds.

She lets out a shock of laughter. "What, Australian?"

"Yeah. I don't know how you can stand it." He softens his tone to say, "That's all I was worried about, in the beginning. I knew you were quite taken with him, and I didn't want you putting your life on hold for some bloke who could have been doing god-knows-what across the world. Or worse, I thought you might rush into a commitment to someone you'd met abroad and didn't know well enough. But maybe," he concedes, "I was letting my own experience colour my opinion there."

"Your experience with *Mamá*, you mean," Androulla says.

"With your mum, yeah. Christ, my friends and I were only in Rhodes for ten days. We went to her parents' taverna one night and I came back, basically, with a wife!" he says.

"You're very different people," Androulla agrees.

"But we had no way of knowing that because our circumstances meant that we had to make a snap decision. So any uncertainty I expressed about your relationship, believe it or not, was coming from a place of concern," Gary says.

Androulla slides her fingers down the beaded cord, giving them friction burn. "Why are you telling me this now? What's changed?"

"Well, I think that conversation with Yannis–"

"Giannis."

"–made me wonder if there were some things I could have been better at, over the years. And that maybe," he says, "it's time we worked on this relationship. What do you think?"

Androulla's fingers fall still.

"Is that something you'd like?"

A snake of dread curls up in her stomach. She wants to pull its head back to strike at her father, with reminders of all the things he got wrong when she was a child and of how little he knows her as an adult. She has a sister that he doesn't recognise. She was raised with a culture that he is unwilling to acknowledge. She may not have Cypriot blood in her veins, but this country filled every room of the house she grew up in and lodged itself deep inside her heart. And yet Gary wonders why she is so stubbornly, clashingly un-English.

In Androulla's primary home, there were no rules about elbows on the dinner table. She wasn't taught to leave the last morsel in every bowl, or to knock on doors before entering and then speak in a low voice. Nor was she told that she should say she was fine 'thank you', if anyone asked. Her mother cooked Greek food, lots of it when people came over, and the more comfortable they made themselves at her table, the better. To leave a crumb uneaten was an insult. Everyone was welcome in every room, at least until Androulla reached a certain age, and no one spoke in a low voice. If they were ever less than 'fine', they said so. No one looked alarmed when Androulla failed to do the courteous thing and lie about her well-being. She, her mother and her stepfather said how they were truthfully. They didn't thank each other for asking, as if to take an interest was to do someone a favour. What kind of message did that send? For Gary to act affronted by behaviour that Androulla didn't understand as rude. She tried to be comfortable with him in the ways she knew how, and by comparison he seemed cold. Perhaps their ways of being were incompatible, and they had never stood a chance.

Androulla watches the beaded cord, still swinging from where she released it. This is a well-worn argument. She and her father both know his shortcomings. But only Androulla knows how she has forsaken him in recent weeks. Despair threatens to drag her to her knees. This is what she has been waiting for since she was a little girl, stirring the cereal around her bowl at Dads' Breakfast while her stepfather sat opposite her, his knees jutting up above her primary school lunch table. Kostas came to the event every year, knowing he wasn't Androulla's first choice and that she would have given anything for her 'real' father to be there. He never let any hurt show, despite what his role in her life must have meant to him since Olympia had suffered an ectopic pregnancy and learned that conceiving again could kill her. Kostas was always there, waiting, patiently, for Androulla to see him. After years, she took on his country and his family. She has taken on his surname, Demetriou, and now look.

As the cord stills, Androulla's guilt turns to indignance. Why does Gary think that he can start parenting her now, when she is in her mid-twenties and married? She imagines him coming to collect her from school, when all her classmates left hours ago. She has sat staring forlornly out the window and now here he is, asking her to pick up her book bag.

"Fuck off," Androulla wants to say to him. She also wants to hug his leg and cry, "I love you, Daddy. Let's go . . ." though she hates herself for it.

She never wants her stepfather to feel that he is not enough, or that he has been just a stand-in for all this time. Kostas is more than Androulla could have asked for, and far more than he was obliged to offer.

"Andy?" her father says, with a hint of nervousness.

In one motion, she wrenches the blind up. Beyond the window, there is only darkness. Androulla hates the idea that blood should matter in who is her parent, more than ever now she fears that she won't share it with her own child.

MAY

THE NINTH

THE FIRST TIME SHE meets with Pantelis is at a coffee shop near the northern border. Androulla skirts past Ledra Street Crossing Point on her way there, and sees the Greek-speaking soldiers inspecting passports in their booths. Beyond the buffer zone, Turkish-speaking soldiers will perform their own checks, neither side trusting the other's authority.

With a look up at the greying sky, Androulla speeds her walk. She arrives at the coffee shop half an hour early, through a side door to its courtyard. The weathered walls are hung with plants, odd tiles and retro soft drinks advertisements. The tables have round, coloured tops and ladder-back chairs set around them. Peering up through the blossoms of a central cherry tree, Androulla decides to take her chances at an unsheltered table. The murmur of voices from inside is faint. She is alone in the courtyard, with only the leaf-rustling breeze and her book for company.

She grips the book tighter as she reads of its characters' struggles for visas. The pages feel thin between her fingers, like they could tear at any turn. At the mention of illegal work, she takes a sharp breath in. And another at the sound of her name.

Pantelis is hovering over her table with a look of uncertainty in his eyes. Recognising their comb-like lashes, Androulla gestures for him to join her.

"*Geiá sas*," the proprietor greets them, taking a notepad and pencil from his apron pocket. "What can I get you?"

Halfway to pulling his chair out, Pantelis stops and orders a coffee with milk and sugars. Androulla asks for plain black.

"Thanks for meeting me," she says, as Pantelis sinks down opposite her.

He smiles, holding onto the sides of his chair as though not finished tucking it in. "What are you reading?" he asks.

Androulla turns the cover of her book to face him. "Do you know it?"

"No," Pantelis says, shaking his head.

"It's about this Nigerian couple . . ." With another spiny breath in, Androulla retracts her hand.

Pantelis brings his elbows to rest on the table and lifts them off as it rocks.

"Oh, here," Androulla says, taking hold of it.

Its metal legs drag onto even paving.

"*Oríste*," the proprietor says, delivering their coffees.

The smell of the sugar in Pantelis's makes Androulla's tongue curl. Steam rises between them.

"Do you mind if I smoke?" he asks.

"No, that's fine," she says.

She watches, envious, as he busies his hands with lighting up.

"So," he strains, through an inhalation, "you wanted to talk about the writing process?"

"Yeah," Androulla says.

Giannis's idea, to get her out and integrating.

"I loved your poems the other week. Especially that one, '*Évreche Símera*'," she pronounces, again. The Cypriot way.

Exhaling smoke, Pantelis thanks her. She tells him the story of which it reminded her, about her great grandfather mocking her 'clean' Greek and nicknaming her *Vréhe*.

"Oh, so you're Greek?" Pantelis responds, sitting up straighter. "Not Cypriot?"

"Not by blood," Androulla admits. "But my stepfather just adopted me. And I grew up with him, so. I've always felt that I'm Cypriot."

"That's nice," Pantelis smiles, revealing his uneven teeth. "And you're a writer?"

"In my spare time. I've come up with something recently, that I think could be taken more seriously? But I don't know." With her face warming, Androulla shrugs.

"As long as you enjoy it, that's the main thing. Especially in Cyprus." Shifting forwards, Pantelis taps his ash into the tray between them.

Androulla frowns. "What do you mean?"

"Well," he says, lifting his eyes.

She follows them up to the gathering clouds.

"There aren't any platforms for Cypriot writers internationally, and barely anyone reads here. A lot of poets self-publish, their families and friends buy their books. And never open them," he says, with a grimace.

"But you performed at that European event," Androulla reminds him.

He sighs. "It's a nice idea, what that organisation is trying to do. But they don't have any money. They invited me to read in Prague once, but they couldn't afford to pay for my flight and neither could I. So that was that."

Androulla waits for him to laugh before she does, at this. The leaves of the cherry tree stir in the breeze.

"I think someone could put Cyprus on the map, though. Like Leonidas Argyrou is trying to do."

Pantelis cocks his head.

"The Cypriot poet. British-born," Androulla adds, when he shows no sign of recognition.

Pantelis asks for the name again so that he can look it up later.

"Like, I have no connection to Nigeria, for example," Androulla goes on, gesturing to her book. "But I'm still enjoying this, because the story is compelling. If someone here could create something like that, then maybe . . ."

"The problem is," Pantelis says, lowering his cigarette, "you need time to write professionally, right? I looked into grants a couple of years ago, and found that the only ones we have here are funded by political parties. Meaning you have to align yourself with one of them, or else there's a ceiling for you."

"And did you?" Androulla asks.

Pantelis sits back, making his chair creak. "Personally, I find both the left and the right too extreme. And I want my work to speak for itself."

"Yeah," she says.

"So I live with my parents, writing poems that no one will read." With a bitter laugh, he taps off his cigarette.

"Do you work at all?" Androulla asks.

"I'm between jobs," Pantelis says, expelling a grey breath, "but I'll find something."

She takes a sip of her coffee.

"How about you?"

"I do some ghostwriting. I don't love it," she admits, lowering her cup. "But I'm in this situation, because of Brexit . . ."

Her saucer gives a warning 'clink'.

At the look of alarm upon Pantelis's face, Androulla wishes she hadn't mentioned this. Migration departments everywhere exist to remind you that you don't belong, that you are an outsider, alien, and your love for their country means nothing without the right colour passport or bankcard. Androulla is unwelcome. She has been questioned by her father and eyed, warily, beside her stepfather. She is aware of it every night that Giannis goes out to work over his permitted twenty hours per week, and her heart sits high up in her chest until he gets home. Soon even his student visa will run out, and they will be apart again for an indeterminate length of time. Both of them have accepted that they must stunt their careers in order to stay here, while their friends in London and Melbourne secure big city jobs with promotions and mortgages. It is a short-term sacrifice, they take turns to remind each other – as they scrape together parking meter change – for long-term fulfilment like none of their peers will ever know. It has to be, because this is home to them both and it is too late to turn back. They have invested too much. Hope, as well as money, for the future of Cyprus and their places within it.

For a year since, Androulla has received every indication that she is a pest. A burden. More trouble than she is worth. At last, she fears she is starting to believe it, and feels all her delusions raining down on her from the darkened sky. She doesn't deserve this, she wants to impress upon Pantelis. To take his hands and make him understand that she isn't a pretender, a nuisance, here to sponge off of the state. Ironically, if she was allowed to work on her 'extended stay', that wouldn't have to be a concern. It is the legal system that is wrought with contradictions, not Androulla. She has things to offer. She could be useful. If she was asked for something – by anyone here – she would do it. Without a second thought, she would prove herself to them.

"That sounds complicated," Pantelis says, with a consolatory smile. "So, where are you staying through all this? With your parents?"

"With my partner," Androulla concedes.

Pantelis's face falls. "Oh," he says, stubbing out his cigarette. "Your partner is Cypriot?"

"He is. Of Cypriot heritage," Androulla says, tucking back her hair. "He grew up in Oakleigh?"

Pantelis shakes his head, sticking out his bottom lip to insert another cigarette. He flicks his lighter into action.

"It's a suburb of Melbourne, Australia. There's a lot of diaspora there," Androulla goes on.

Pantelis is looking away from her, at a group of three girls who have just walked in. They are wearing short shorts and cropped tops, despite the fact that it is only May and the sky is turning greyer by the minute. Tourists.

"He's got visa stuff on-going too," Androulla says, to pull Pantelis's attention back. "He'll probably be gone most of this summer."

As though her presence has just occurred to him, Pantelis turns back.

She shrugs. "So, we'll see what happens."

"It's like that?" he says, with a trace of hope returning to the corners of his lips.

At the thought of Giannis leaving, Androulla feels a pang. "Not exactly. I mean, we've talked about trying, kind of, a more open relationship."

Pantelis nods, slowly. "I've never met anyone in an open relationship."

"Really?" Androulla asks. As if she has.

"I suggested the idea to a girlfriend once," Pantelis recalls, with a faint smile. He raises his eyebrows. "It didn't go down well."

Laughing, Androulla asks why not.

"She was already done with me, I think. Cheating. I was just trying to give her an out." He shrugs.

"I'm sorry," Androulla says.

He shakes his head. "It was a long time ago."

"Are you with anyone now?" she asks, lifting her coffee cup.

She can see his answer over its rim. The way that he looks at her sends her stomach lurching as though from a perilous height.

"No," Pantelis confirms.

The sky opens up, sending the cherries bobbing and their blossoms wincing. Dropping her cup down, Androulla stows her book in her tote bag. Pantelis drops his cigarette into the ashtray and they take shelter inside the coffee shop.

"Shall we . . ?"

"Yeah, I think that's our cue. It was nice talking to you, anyway," Androulla says, over the tourists' shrieking.

"And you," Pantelis says, ignoring the girls as they fuss, cups in hand, across the courtyard. "We should do this again."

Androulla smiles. "That would be nice."

September

THE THIRTEENTH

"READY?" ANDROULLA ASKS.

Stopping mid-step, Giannis looks to the window and back again. "You seriously want to go out, in this?"

"We have to," Androulla insists. "It's tradition, your first night back."

The wind changes direction, throwing daggers of rain into the glass.

"Come on." She opens the door.

Giannis bends to lace up his trainers.

It is too hot for raincoats. They agree this wordlessly, staring out of their building's entranceway. Yellow chrysanthemums twitch upon impact, until those with the longest stems fold over themselves. Pulling the door open, Androulla smells the damp earth. Rain only falls this thick after a drought, with the heat of summer still held in the ground. It demands more, and the heavens oblige. Androulla steps outside.

"No," Giannis starts.

She hears him pounding after her, around the building and to their car. Their shoulders heave side by side in the front seat.

"That wasn't so bad," Androulla says, folding her sun visor down to inspect her makeup. Heavy on the brows and eyelids, with a bold red lip. Satisfied, she pushes the mirror back to the ceiling.

Giannis starts the engine without returning her smile.

As they drive into the city centre, she peers through the rain to see Nicosia as she imagines he is seeing it, for the first time in almost four months. Hung with golden fairy lights as if for Christmas. Choked with cars, either trembling in traffic or cutting each other up at amber signals. Slamming on the breaks, Giannis curses. While he was in Australia awaiting his new student visa, Androulla spent time out of town, too. On the coast, mostly, first sending him selfies that she smiled for with her girl-friends. Then instructing those girl-friends to take pictures of her alone, with one hip stuck out and a sultry expression, in a series of smaller and stringier bikinis. By August she was posing topless for her previously dormant Instagram, and feeling her heart skip when Giannis's friends viewed the photos. That meant he was seeing them, even once he had deactivated his account.

He doesn't join her in laughing off the rain when they reach the restaurant, on the edge of Eleftheria Square.

"Let's sit here," she says, stopping at a table out front.

Lightning flashes white across the sky, as if to animate Giannis's protest.

"There's no one else out here," he implores her.

"It's fine. Look, we're completely sheltered," she says, gesturing at the broad wooden awning overhead. "You don't just want to sit where everyone else is sitting, do you?"

Giannis makes no further argument as he takes the seat opposite her. He goes inside to place their order, and to pick it up on a grubby tray when the buzzer goes off between them.

"Those things are so aggressive," Androulla chortles, over the rain.

The smell of chicken and pork *souvlákia* rises, for once drawing no stray cats. Androulla mixes her salad, a cardboard tray of cucumber, tomato, red onion and feta, which thickens in her mouth. She picks around it.

"So, how's everyone in Oakleigh?" she asks, despite the video calls in which Giannis updated her, live on-site.

He repeats the news from his friends and family members without looking up from his pork. While he pulls the meat, a piece at a time, from its skewer, Androulla nods and asks more questions to which she already knows the answers. Her husband becomes no livelier as he sips his beer. She does lots of cutting and pushing around of the heartier food on her plastic plate, lots of lifting and lowering her fork as if taken by something he has said. She drinks wolfishly, spilling lager down her chin. The glow from the window behind Giannis is disrupted only by the shocks of electricity that Androulla senses over her shoulder. She pulses the ball of her foot upon the ground.

"Today was fun," she reminds him.

As though oblivious to her suggestive tone, he crosses his knife and fork over his plate.

On the drive home, Androulla turns up the radio so she can feel its bass lines reverberating. "This makes me want to go out-out," she says, nodding along.

Giannis looks sideways at her, and she knows she isn't the girl that he married mere months ago. But this is what marriage is, the stubbornness in her maintains. It is growing and changing with someone. She keeps nodding until they get home.

Hanging his keys up inside the front door, Giannis faces her. "We should probably talk."

"Now?" Androulla whines, rolling up the hem of his T-shirt. He stills her hand. "Yes."

"But we've just done so much talking," she persists.

"Not about August, we haven't. I said, stop." He pushes her. Stumbling backwards, she stares at him. "Yes, we have."

"Over the phone. That's not the same," he maintains, tucking his T-shirt back over his belt.

Androulla's thumbnail hurts where he tore it away from the buckle. She spreads her hands. "Talk then, if you want to talk. I've got nothing to say."

"Nothing," Giannis repeats. "Not, sorry? Still?"

"What is it I'm supposed to be sorry for?"

At his scoff, she spreads her hands wider.

"Why don't we start from when Naomi got here? So I can see how your story checks out," he mutters.

"Right. If that's how this conversation is going to go," Androulla says, turning away.

Giannis follows her into the living room. She hears his footsteps behind her and braces her palms upon the table, not looking back. There is a vicious 'ping' before the light comes on overhead, and she sees herself reflected in the darkened window. Giannis looms behind her.

"This conversation isn't going to go anywhere, if you keep walking away from me," he says, stopping still. He sighs. "I know what you did. I just don't understand what you were thinking."

Androulla's hands curl into fists, her engagement ring scratching across the tabletop. "You know exactly what I was thinking. You were thinking the same thing," she says, through gritted teeth. "Before you went to Australia, we agreed. We had no idea how long we were going to be apart, and it might just have made the distance more bearable if we opened things up a bit. You wanted it, Gianni. So don't pretend–"

He sneers, "I didn't want it like that."

"You didn't want it to be me, you mean," Androulla snaps, rounding on him. "It was the hottest thing in the world when you were flirting with that girl at your gym. But Naomi and I had one night out in Agia Napa, and you couldn't hack it."

"A night out, is that what you're calling it? Androulla, you could have gotten yourself killed," Giannis says, wide-eyed. "Naomi's probably scarred for life–"

"Naomi is fine," Androulla growls. "You don't even know what happened. You said you wanted me to be honest. And I was," she adds, before he can interrupt. "But you weren't listening. Otherwise, there's no way you'd be talking to me like this."

Giannis falls back a step. "Tell me what happened, then. I'm listening," he says. "Tell me how you auditioned for work in a strip club. You fucked some sunburned Brit on the beach at three a.m. while your husband was across the world, spending every minute of every day trying to get back to you, and yet you're the victim. Tell me how."

"That's not . . ." Androulla shakes her head. "First of all, I didn't fuck anyone. All I did was go down to the beach, and that guy . . ."

Tears prick her eyes and she turns back to the window. The sky flashes white, illuminating her stricken face and Giannis's reflection shifting closer. She watches his hand move, stiffly, upwards. When he touches her arm, she jerks away.

"What . . ?"

"I've told you, I don't want to talk about this," she says, shouldering past him.

"Androulla–"

"We said we wouldn't mind each other hooking up with other people, as long as there were no emotions involved. Right?"

she says, looking back from the doorway with blinked-dry eyes. "And the only emotions I see here are yours."

Giannis drops his hands. "I don't care what happened with the guy. You're right, we said we were fine with that stuff. What bothers me is the rest of it. You getting that drunk, in an area that notorious. Getting yourself and Naomi locked in a basement with some kind of pimp, saying you wanted a job . . ."

"It was a joke," Androulla says, rolling her eyes.

"What kind of joke is that?" Giannis asks, his face twisted. "Who laughed?"

"We did," she says, with an illustrative snort. "It was funny. All we did was arrive at the club ten minutes early, and they told us we had to come back later. Unless we were there for a job."

"And you thought it was okay to say yes to that, when you had Naomi with you?" Giannis takes a step closer. "You used to be so protective, and you put her in direct danger that night."

Androulla turns sharply into their bedroom, letting the door swing shut behind her.

Giannis bats it open. "You're not right, Androulla."

"Yes, you've made that clear," she says.

"That's not what I mean. The way you've acted this summer . . ."

She looks at their rumpled bed sheets, their clothes from last night when Giannis got in – and from this morning – discarded in piles across the floor. Ten times in twenty-four hours. That must be a record, even for them. It would be naïve to think that none of the urgency with which they have torn at each other, through the last day and night, had been fuelled by fear. By the knowledge that once they had exhausted themselves physically, they would have to face this confrontation. Androulla feels her heart thumping, adrenaline coursing through her body. It ends up where it always does, in a pulse of testosterone at her groin. She could go again, but her husband is depleted. Biology, back to confound her. She feels her skin stretching away from her eyes, her senses heightened beyond detecting the eucalyptus scent restored to their room. This is how she has been living for weeks, off of animal instinct. She feels alert. She feels free.

"You look thin," Giannis says.

Androulla affects a smile. "Thank you."

"You didn't eat much at dinner."

"What, are you monitoring me now?"

"I'm worried about you. Which is just about the only reason I'm still here," he says, jabbing a finger at her. "We might have had an arrangement this summer. But you, the normal you, wouldn't refuse to say sorry for hurting my feelings because of a technicality. You're supposed to be empathetic. You're supposed to be thoughtful, and actually cautious to the point of annoying, sometimes. Not this crazy, reckless person."

"Yeah. Well, I'm also supposed to be Cypriot. And married to a Cypriot. And able to have kids, and look how all of that's turned out," Androulla slurs. She blinks, realising how hard the alcohol must have hit her unlined stomach.

Giannis retracts his finger. "I thought you weren't bothered about the kid thing," he says.

"Wouldn't matter if I was, would it," Androulla retorts. She expels a short breath, then says, "I'm sorry you feel hurt, Gianni. I didn't think I was out of line, given the conversations we'd had this spring. But obviously, you disagree."

"Is that what you want to do here?" he asks, standing back. "Agree to disagree?"

Androulla shrugs, holding her eyebrows high in defiance.

"Right," Giannis says. He runs a hand through his hair. "I'm going to brush my teeth."

OCTOBER

THE TWELFTH

"SEE YOU LATER," GIANNIS mumbles, on his way out the front door.

"Bye," Androulla calls. She doesn't look up from her laptop.

The door thuds shut and she hears his footsteps growing quieter down the echoing stairwell, then nothing. Her screen looks brighter. On it is a Word document, letters sprawling across the page to form words, sentences, paragraphs. They surge from her fingertips without her consciously choosing them, as though from some shadow side of her brain. In order to engage it, she must first disengage from the world around her. There can be no thinking, no texting, no talking.

This has been easy in the last month or so. Since she and Giannis agreed to disagree about her antics in August, their apartment has been quiet. As a result, Androulla's latest story is growing a thousand words longer each day. The conditions are perfect. Any obligation that she once felt to sit with her husband of an evening, to play a game or watch a film, has gone. There is no pressure from him, either. Androulla still goes to bed with him, but only for twenty minutes of callous distraction. There is no build-up beforehand and no hanging around afterwards. She returns to their rickety round table and writes through the night.

The rain is pummelling down outside, creating an effect like white noise. Androulla tunes into it, losing track of her fingers as they fly across the keyboard. She flicks her eyes up to the screen. There has been no paragraph break – no full stop, even – for some time. She feels powerless to disrupt the story as it flows through her. The setting, Cyprus, is luminescent. Androulla has titled the document 'Copper', since that has been the element most mined in this country, historically. That has stained the soil red. That has retreated deeper into the Troodos Mountains over millennia, and those pursuing it have gouged greater steps into the mountainsides to chase it down.

Beginning a new line with speech marks, Androulla pauses. The one instance in which she does have to think, with this story, is when her protagonist speaks. Ariadne is the girl's name, meaning 'most holy', and it suits her. Newly emergent from her sheltered upbringing, she is the most unworldly character that Androulla has devised to date. With little knowledge and no opinions, despite having grown up in Cyprus, Ariadne trawls the streets of Nicosia in a kind of dream-state. Making money is of no importance to her. Instead, she is driven forward by a desire to understand the troubles of her home country. She is funded by her parents, to keep the focus on what she learns of the mysterious, Turkish-occupied north, and of herself through exploring it. For once, this artlessness makes for a compelling story. The contrast between the character's simplicity and the setting's complexity is staggering, Androulla thinks. At last, after years of missing the mark, she has done it. She has figured out how to write a readable book.

The thrill that bubbles up in her stomach simmers down to dread, just briefly. With a long breath out, Androulla puts aside her feelings on the Cyprus Problem. For it is Ariadne's turn to speak now, and she has yet to form any. It doesn't matter that Androulla detests even the term 'the Cyprus Problem', which suggests it should concern no one else. It doesn't matter how she aches for her grandparents, who lost their home in the north and who doubt they will ever receive compensation. Or how she fears for her very pretty, Turkish-speaking friend walking home at night, when the streetlights on her side of the city do not work. Ariadne will come to understand that there are horrors on both sides of the border, that there were no winners in the conflict of nineteen-seventy-four. But not yet. That is the big reveal, and must wait until the end of the book.

In the meantime, Androulla has her say, "Really? What do you mean? Wow, I'd never looked at it that way before . . ."

She holds Ariadne back from expressing preferences on what to eat and who to sleep with. Ariadne is aware of her weight, but not plagued by thoughts of it when she sits down to dinner. Any sex that she has is boring, uninspired by what Androulla has done or seen online. Except perhaps on the channels that she started off watching, and graduated from some time ago now. Nothing excites her more than inhabiting Ariadne's innocence. In the last few months, Androulla's own thoughts and behaviours have become so depraved that she needs the escape more than ever. By comparison, Ariadne's dullness is a thrill. Like how the rain falling outside is such a rarity in Cyprus – and so needed after the summer – that it is 'good weather'. What sets Ariadne apart is that the story unfolding around her is interesting. Perhaps interesting enough to be published, Androulla thinks. Never again will she have to write on behalf of faceless foodies, while her stomach cries out and she refuses to indulge it.

The rain slows, its change of pitch breaking Androulla's concentration. She sits back. The room has turned dark around her laptop, she realises, and she gets up to switch on a light. She stretches the stiffness from her legs and blinks her eyes used to its yellow glow. Deprived of food and sleep, her body is on high alert. She hears its demands and feels detached enough to say which should be denied, including the growling of her stomach and the heaviness of her eyelids. The throbbing between her legs, she pauses over. This sensation is one that Androulla cannot work through. It will block her creative mind from functioning until she has seen it off. It always does. She checks her phone. Ten p.m. and no word from Giannis. Perhaps his meeting has overrun, or he has gone on for a drink with the others in his department. Androulla doubts he will be much longer if that is the case. Peer relationships at the doctorate level sound very different to those at under or even post-graduate. Resolving to wait for him, she resumes her seat at the table.

As she feared, her body is too restless for any real writing now. She cannot tune her mind back to the frequency of the rain, even to read over what she has already written. Closing the 'Copper' document, she breaks the rule designed to keep her nights sacred and logs onto work. She adds a few lines to one of her on-going projects, a work of 'non-fiction' depicting various conspiracy theories. What Androulla does for money is typing, she has decided, not writing. As the night persists, her focus on lizard people and the secret Nazi headquarters lurking beneath Denver Airport makes her feel crazy. She shuts down her laptop. One a.m., her phone says, and still no Giannis.

Androulla lifts a hand to her head. Perhaps her husband isn't on campus tonight, but at the bar. For all her waking nights and skipping meals, she might have lost track of the days. Assuming that he won't be home for another couple of hours, she takes herself to bed, turning off lights as she goes. Sleep eludes her, even after she has answered her body's demands twice. It is her mind that is restless now, returning to her father's absence, Oscar's death, her inability to create life and live hers to the fullest where she wants to, the links between all these things and, finally, their convergence in Agia Napa. The summer has passed, Androulla reassures herself, with a rustle of the duvet that they have just started sleeping with again this month. She pulls it down to feel that there are no stranger's hands around her neck.

Opens her eyes to see that there are no headlights bearing out of the darkness. Her feet are relaxed, not aching from her six-hour walk along the highway to escape the Mancunian holidaymaker who had been blowing cigarette smoke into her face all night, the lesser of his crimes. She is safe. There is just the drubbing of the rain outside, and the forest-like scent on the pillow beside hers.

Three a.m. arrives without her husband. The rain stops, as if to abandon Androulla with the realisation that wherever Giannis began the night, in working or studying pursuit of their brighter future, he has not ended it there. He has stayed out to do his bit for their long-distance strategy, at last. Despite being back together, they have never been further apart. Androulla sits up in bed and hugs her knees, letting them go before her body can misinterpret this posture as a cue to round forward, to tremble or leak tears. There is no need for that. She has no right to be upset. And, actually, she doesn't think she is. She turns Giannis's pillow over to stop his scent from rising. If anything, she thinks, this will be a good leveller. A restoration of her husband's pride. A reminder to him that sex is just sex. They always said so, didn't they? Hypothetically.

While Giannis was away, Androulla had this theory confirmed by two more doctors, both of whom made the same bizarre translation as the first. She would never 'catch' a baby. Her acne medication hasn't quelled her swollen lymph node, but apparently that is of no concern. Her skin looks better than ever and is making her quite vain. She hasn't told Giannis that she is even less hopeful of passing it on to a child now, along with his warm eyes and her terrible food habits, than she was after her first scan. That would take the fun out of things, and she is the only one of 'the boys's' partners not to have bored or scared them with talk of a baby yet. They are all jealous of how cool Androulla is, Giannis tells her. And of how good-looking.

Knowing this gives Androulla a rush of enough self-esteem that it feels like a turn-on. Perhaps it is. Perhaps she can only be fulfilled by lots of attention from numerous people. She isn't causing trouble after all, but troubled. Would that feel better? She sighs to fill the silence left in the wake of the rain. So much of life is in how you frame things, she thinks. Just last week, she saw a headline announcing that yet another Disney Kid had come out as polyamorous. 'Come out', suggesting that their desire to have multiple partners at the same time was a sexuality, a preference they were born with and could not control, rather than a lifestyle choice. Androulla wouldn't claim to know better, but the difference in implication does interest her. If acting upon attractions to other people is a behavioural choice, or a lack of discipline, then she has failed and betrayed her husband. But if it is as fundamental to her being as, say, homosexuality is to some, then she is a victim. Oppressed, by contemporary western standards, confined to the cage of monogamy by a stale and domineering man. She should free herself.

But she loves him, she thinks, as he drifts off to sleep in the arms of another, invisible woman. And the fact is, none of this matters. Neither one of them can hold the other accountable because this is something they agreed to experiment with. It has all been trial and error. No, not error, Androulla soothes herself, as the memory of August tightens its grip on her neck again. It has been trial and . . . Her collarbones feel cold to the touch. She cannot think of another word.

The Twenty-First

A CAR HORN BEEPS twice, just as Androulla's phone chimes. Sharing her essay on attachment theory with the student who will take credit for it, she shuts her laptop and leaves her apartment.

As suspected, a light drizzle is falling on her parents' Ford Focus. Climbing into the backseat, Androulla expels a sigh.

"Hello," her mother greets her, craning around.

"Hey. Thanks for doing this," Androulla says, leaning her head back. "Three assignments due this morning . . . I don't know how I managed that."

Olympia's lips are shimmering pink, her floral perfume filling the car. "Look what's here," she says, in a sing-song voice.

Androulla catches her stepfather's eye in the rear view mirror.

"Next to you," he says, flicking his indicator on.

She turns. On the seat beside her is a rectangular box, ivory with a texture like the veins of a leaf running across it. Androulla catches her breath. She draws her hands into her lap, afraid that to touch the object might be to shrivel and dry it to ash.

"Isn't that box beautiful? It matches the cover of the album, apparently," Olympia says, as they pull off the kerb.

The indicator ceases its ticking.

"That's nice," Androulla mumbles. Catching Kostas's eye again, she gives an overzealous nod. "I'm excited to open it. But we should wait for Giannis."

Her heart thuds, heavily, for the ten-minute drive to her grandparents' house, past the ice cream shop that was her favourite as a child. Androulla stares through the window, envying the people inside their immunity to the guilt that would cripple her now. At a green light, Kostas turns down a side street, away from the Limassol Road by which he used to take her to the sea. Androulla travelled it countless times this summer, alone.

There is no pavement outside her grandparents' white, dusty-shuttered bungalow, just a steel gate that shrieks open at her touch. Iron spokes stick up from the flat roof, like green shoots from the earth. These are 'rods of hope' that Androulla's parents, or perhaps Androulla, will build her life up from their home. By what means, she cannot imagine.

"*Kaliméra sas,*" her grandmother says, opening her arms as wide as the door. "Welcome." Her grey-brown hair is fragrant with cooking smells, her embrace full-bodied and warm.

"*Geiá sou, Pappoú,*" Androulla greets her grandfather, in turn.

He lands a clumsy kiss upon her cheek, almost catching her mouth.

Androulla giggles. Her grandparents have lived in this house for years longer than there has been a Limassol Road, or an office block called The Asteroid to desecrate the view from their garden. Between his career in genetics and hers as a midwife, they were able to have it built for themselves and their three children. Despite those same careers, they were able to accept Androulla for as true a grandchild as their son Stavros' and daughter Chrystalla's biological children, from the year they met her. Androulla stands back.

Wiping his shirt sleeve across his glasses, her grandfather asks, "Are those the photos?"

She looks down at the box, indecently sparkly amid the drizzle.

"Yes." Her smile feels hollow.

"Let's get them inside," her grandmother says, ushering Kostas and Olympia in after her.

They settle in the living room, where Androulla rests the box upon a lace-covered coffee table. Picture frames stud a sideboard, their glass inserts smeared with fingerprints. Despite the glare of the yellow ceiling light, Androulla knows who they depict.

"We invited your cousins," her grandmother says, glancing over her shoulder, "but they couldn't make it, unfortunately. We'll have to arrange another celebration, also for Christina's engagement."

"Oh, yes," Olympia says, brightly.

Androulla draws her knees together. The room feels full as it is, with both her parents and her grandfather squeezed onto a two-person sofa. Androulla and her grandmother are hip-to-hip on an adjacent one, and have yet to fit Giannis on.

"Another time," Androulla murmurs.

The doorbell pierces the air.

She feels each one of her grandmother's footsteps echo through her chest, then a shrinking sensation at the sound of Giannis's voice.

"*Kaliméra sas,*" he says, coming around the living room doorway.

Androulla's grandfather stands to shake his hand, asking, "*Ti káneis?*"

"Good. Busy morning," Giannis says. "I had some things to catch up on at school . . ."

While he answers her parents' follow-up questions, Androulla dares to look at him. Not through him, as she has been doing, to screen out his familiarity. She determines that his stubble is three days old and reacquaints herself with the curve of his wrist bone, sticking out from his trouser pocket.

A rattling precedes her grandmother's return, with a tray of Cypriot Coffee cups. One with sugar for Androulla's grandfather. Three without for Giannis, Kostas and Androulla. Then her grandmother fetches chamomile teas for herself and Olympia, and extra side tables to put them on.

"No drinks on the coffee table," she rules, catching Androulla's eye. "This album is too precious!"

Androulla forces a smile, staring at the box whose contents her parents paid for and which she knows is already tainted. It smells both woody and chemical under the lid, like a tree that someone has varnished.

"It does match," Olympia marvels, as Androulla folds the cover back.

It creaks.

"Careful . . ."

Before she can glare at her mother, coos of delight come tumbling over Androulla's shoulders. Her relatives lean in, warming her ears with praise for the opening spread. On one page, a close-up of joined hands. On the other, 'Androulla and Giannis' with their wedding date in a looping script. Androulla's arms feel like lead. With great effort, she turns the page.

"Wow," her grandfather says, shifting closer.

Olympia traces the album's edge with her forefinger. "These are gorgeous," she murmurs.

Androulla studies the pictures of herself in her parents' living room, with one woman styling her hair and another painting her face. She is perched on a chair between them, wrapped in a towel dressing gown. In the background, a violinist is playing.

"Not that one," she responds, to a photo taken before her spots were powdered over.

"You look beautiful," her grandmother protests, "smiling at your friend."

Androulla looks again. As her *kouméra*, her maid of honour, Naomi wore a satin dress they had agreed upon, rather than doing herself the typically English disservice of too floral a pattern for her pale skin. Androulla had her cousins and other family members to get ready with her. But all her friends came from London, since she had yet to make any in Cyprus.

Giannis is surrounded by Cypriots in his dressing photos, men from his course and the bar in their twenties and thirties, with shot glasses of zivania in hand. They take turns to shave his beard, as is custom, while a lutist plays. Most of Giannis's friends from Melbourne are missing, since it is a longer and less affordable journey from there to Cyprus. Still he is grinning, broadly.

Androulla turns the page and there is a collective intake of breath. She takes its bottom-right corner between her finger and thumb, but her relatives want to stop and relive the moment when she met Giannis outside the venue. To tilt their heads and point out the adoration in his eyes as he extended his hand, and invited Androulla to walk up the aisle with him. Her giddy smile as she accepted. The paper is too glossy, Androulla decides, as they proceed to the altar – or to the table that they had in place of one. A sheen obscures their faces as they gaze into each other's eyes, and does not clear no matter how she angles the album beneath the ceiling light.

"Are you okay?" Kostas asks.

"Yeah, it's just . . ." Androulla starts, frowning upwards.

Rubbing her eyes, she senses Giannis sitting motionless on the other side of her grandmother. The images are clearer now. In one of her making her vows, Androulla tries to find what she was thinking. Dressed like a princess in her ball gown and golden tiara, when she had always hated Britain's colonialism for tearing Cyprus apart. With a new band on her ring finger, though she had grown up saying that she would never marry. What was the point? Her parents had done it and then divorced. Perhaps it was Kostas's goodness that had restored her faith, over the years. Perhaps she had met the right person. She was devastated that she and Giannis couldn't sign the papers that day, if she wanted to preserve her claim to Cypriot citizenship by descendancy. And now?

Androulla touches the bottom-left photograph, where Giannis's suit jacket trails off. Naomi has a gay housemate who says that monogamy is outdated, a practice rooted in the history of men treating women as objects. He thinks of marriage as nothing more than a transaction – it is, traditionally – the handing over of a woman from father to husband. Weddings are perverted affairs. Attending them is no better than slowing down to stare at a three-car pile-up on the motorway. Queer people aren't anchored down by traditions like that, because they weren't allowed to have any until recently. Thank god, the housemate laughs.

Androulla sits back. These ideas made sense when Naomi repeated them to her, in August. But she doesn't recall feeling anchored down on the day of her wedding. Anxious for it to run smoothly, perhaps, self-conscious about standing up in front of so many people and having her picture taken. Yet safe in the folds of the dress that Giannis had said she looked most beautiful in, instead of the low-cut or cinched-tight designs that she had fretted about being in shape for, months earlier. Glowing in the makeup that she'd had professionally done, even before her skin had cleared up. Before the diagnosis that had thrown her so much further off course than she could have imagined, and her relationship with her. Androulla remembers feeling an inordinate sense of calm as she pledged herself to Giannis. A rightness. A quiet, steady joy.

"That's a lovely one," her mother points, over her shoulder. "You should get that framed."

"We should get some also," her grandmother says.

"Yes. We'll all choose our favourites," Olympia agrees.

The rain drips, languidly, down the window.

As she nods along, Androulla feels Giannis watching her. She cannot bring herself to look up. All the tension in her jaw and shoulders, she holds onto until they get home. Then she takes it, balled up into fury, and thrusts it at her husband through gritted teeth.

"I want you to hurt me," she says.

And he agrees.

The Twenty-Second

"Hey," Naomi answers her phone.

Androulla catches her breath. A pine-scent needles her throat as she says, "Hello."

She is standing at the edge of a clearing in her local park, watching a light rain fall. In the spring, she saw a Sri Lankan team playing cricket here, though it isn't a large space. A square, dirt field fenced in by evergreens, with a graffiti-marred bench in one corner. Androulla considers sitting down, but the bench looks wet and she cannot think of being still.

"Are you okay?" Naomi asks.

Androulla's nod sends the hood of her raincoat shrieking against her sleeve. "I'm good, yeah. Sorry." She sniffs. "How are you?"

"I'm fine. What's going on?" Naomi persists.

"Nothing, really. I just . . ." Even as Androulla turns her face, she remains trapped inside her hood with Naomi, the world

113

outside insurmountably large and drizzling. She turns her face back. "I think it's just hit me, like, what I've actually done."

"What do you mean? Like, the stuff in Agia Napa?" Naomi asks.

"Yeah. I know it's taken me a couple of months, but ... I'm so disappointed in myself." A sob breaks from Androulla's chest.

"Oh, Andy," her sister responds.

"Sorry," she says, in a high voice.

"Don't be silly, you've got nothing to apologise for," Naomi assures her.

"Well, I have. That's the point." Androulla manages a hollow laugh.

"Has something happened to change your mind about that?" her sister asks.

"Nothing specific," Androulla says, pulling her voice level. "I think it's just sunk in over time."

"Yeah," Naomi says. "I only ask because you were quite adamant ..."

"I know." Androulla squeezes her eyes shut. "I was so hung up on the technicality, that the open thing was something Giannis and I had agreed to try, I wasn't sorry that I'd hurt him. I wasn't seeing it," she says, reopening her eyes. "Or I was, but I wasn't reacting the way I should have. I don't want this to sound like an excuse but, looking back, I honestly don't think I've felt an emotion. For months."

"It doesn't sound like an excuse," Naomi says. "You've been dissociating."

At the snap of a twig, Androulla looks up. On the other side of the clearing, a man is striding the pine-carpeted path with his head bowed, his arms swinging. A pit bull trots, soundlessly, beside him. Androulla watches them go through the trees. The idea of disconnecting from her feelings, her memories and her identity, consciously, is not alien to her. It is her body that has felt overlarge and isolating for the last few months, like a space-suit. It is as if Androulla has been watching herself rather than being. Does that explain her reckless behaviour, her fearlessness of any consequences? Perhaps Naomi will know. They both had therapy after Oscar's death, for their parents' fears that the ghost of his unhappiness might haunt them, that the plague they had failed to catch when he was alive was one they could not bury with him. Androulla went to sessions for a year, before she understood what a stretch they were for her parents and said that she felt fine. Naomi hasn't left the therapy room, just crossed to the professionals' side of it to get her degree and help other young people.

She is the only person, other than Giannis, who knows about the six-week period five years ago, in which Androulla forgot herself. It was when she was working at the estate agent's, having dreams so close to reality that she couldn't tell them apart. At a nudge from a colleague, she found herself in the office without remembering how she had got there. They had called her name three times, they said, and she hadn't responded. Androulla, she repeated under her breath, trying to connect the sound with herself. She was afraid of telling anyone that she couldn't. Her colleagues went from chuckling along to shooting her strange looks, as this went on. And then it stopped, abruptly. Androulla woke up.

"You haven't been yourself," Naomi insists. "It was like I was talking to a different person in August, and on the phone since then. It's been a bit scary, honestly."

Androulla's phone feels light in her hand. "The fact that you were scared by a situation I put you in . . . I can't believe I did that to you."

"Andy, I know you feel like you should be more responsible because you're older than me. But I am an adult," Naomi reminds her.

Androulla nods, gulping back tears. "I know you are, and I don't mean to sound condescending–"

"I think you need to be less hard on yourself. And remember, we actually haven't stopped laughing about that night since it happened. Moments of it were fucking hilarious."

"Only because we survived," Androulla protests.

Her gasps turn giggling as Naomi recalls what a big game they had talked about going to Nissi Beach, only to lose their nerve at the foam party. It was four p.m., giving them one hour to get drunk enough that they would brave it. How unlikely it was that a middle-aged man should have flopped down at their table afterwards – two girls, alone at a beach bar – and given them flyers from a nearby strip club. How absurd that they went. How obscene that when they walked in to find the lights on, the manager looked at them – still with their short skirts and bikini tops clinging with foam and sweat and sea – and asked if they wanted jobs. None of Naomi's friends can believe that they said yes, for fun.

"I said yes, you mean," Androulla cuts in. "I'm the one who got us locked in that room."

"Was I any better? Smoking the manager's cigarettes, one after another," Naomi says. "I don't even think I asked him."

"No. But I was the one asking questions," Androulla says. "'How long have you run this place? Oh, it was your father's and your brother's before yours? What a nice family business . . .'" she mocks herself. "And then laughing in his face. God, I really thought I was charming him."

"I can't believe he didn't break our kneecaps," Naomi laughs.

Halfway to joining her, Androulla stops. "See, this is what I mean. We're only laughing because it's shocking that we got out okay. We shouldn't have, when you think about it. Especially since the way we got out was with a group of strange boys."

"Strange is an understatement," Naomi says. She takes a breath, as if to say something else, then lets it go. "How do you feel now, about what happened with Seb?"

Androulla's frown dissolves as she remembers that Seb was the name of the boy whose holiday villa they went back to. With whom she walked forty minutes to the beach in the night, leaving Naomi alone with the other two boys. She lifts up her foot and places it back. This ground was hard and cracked in the summer, but now has some give.

"I've been thinking about it," she says. "I still can't remember what his face looked like. Only the shape of him walking next to me, if that makes sense."

"Is that all?" Naomi asks.

Pressing her foot down harder, Androulla watches the pine needles splay out around it.

"We don't have to talk about it, if you don't want to," Naomi adds.

"It's okay." Looking up at the clouds, framed by treetops, Androulla starts across the clearing. "I don't think there's much I haven't told you. We walked a long way to the beach."

"What did you talk about?" Naomi asks.

Without the shelter of the trees, the rain patters down on Androulla's hood.

"It was very sexual," she admits.

"And when you got there, did you . . ?"

"That's the thing, I don't know," she says. "It seems like we should have, it was heading that way. But all I can remember is being on his back in the water, realising I was a long way from shore and too drunk to swim on my own. Even then, it was like it wasn't happening to me, or like I wasn't understanding the danger. I just kept laughing." She shakes her head.

"And you don't remember him touching you?"

"Not then," she says. "But I've told you what happened on the way back to the house."

"Yeah. I mean, you were still kind of laughing about that as well, when you told me," Naomi says, gently.

At the edge of the clearing, Androulla stops. She sees the footprints left by the man with the pit bull, and turns the other way down the path. Sheltered by trees again, there is only the sound of her breath, amplified inside her hood.

"We were just talking. He said I reminded him of his ex, and I remember thinking then, okay. That's a warning sign. We were walking along the highway at that point. And he grabbed my hair and pulled me into the middle of it," she says.

Despite having heard this before, Naomi catches her breath.

"He started strangling me, saying all this stuff in my ear about how if a car came, he'd just leave me there. It was, like, three in the morning, so there was no one around. But then I saw headlights."

"How did you get out of that?" Naomi asks.

Androulla steps over a fallen pinecone. "I pretended to like it," she says. "I thought that if I screamed or seemed scared in any way, it could spook him into doing something worse."

"It's lucky you thought of that. Especially that drunk," Naomi murmurs.

"I needed him. If I ran, I'd have had no idea where I was or how to get back to the house. So I just had to play along with him the rest of the way."

"He did it again, didn't he?" Naomi says.

"Not on the highway. But on a smaller road, yeah," Androulla says. She scoffs. "And then he slammed my head against a wall and kissed me." It feels more like a dream than a memory as she recounts it, like something that happened to someone else. And still the fear grips her, "I can remember before and after, but not what happened on the beach. I can remember the conversations I had with him, but not what he looked like. It doesn't make sense. What if my brain is blocking stuff out to protect me? That happens to people, doesn't it? When they've been through something traumatic."

"This might sound like a strange thing to take comfort in," Naomi says, slowly, "but based on how violent he was, I don't think you'd be unsure if you'd had sex with him. I think you'd have known about it, after."

Androulla rounds a corner to where the pine needles grow sparser, the dirt path more visible. "I hadn't thought of that," she says, looking up.

This clearing houses a large, low-walled pool. It has been emptied since Androulla was a child, visiting in summertime and splashing around with her cousins. She walks its perimeter, watching the rain fill it up with puddles of new, dirty water.

"How much of this does Giannis know?" Naomi asks.

"I told him everything on the phone the next day. You were there," Androulla reminds her. "But that's when it all felt sur-real, still. I told it like a funny story, so everything about us going home with those guys from the strip club, me going off to the beach with one of them . . . It must have sounded like I was asking for something to happen. And I probably was, at first," she admits.

"You flirting with someone does not give them the right to put their hands on you like that," Naomi says, firmly. "We had to walk six hours back to Agia Napa, at four a.m. You stress-fractured all of your toes. Seb threatened to kill you, Androulla."

"But I can't get upset about any of that," Androulla says, stopping still, "because I chose to put myself in the situation, and that hurt Giannis. He thinks he's the victim here. And he is," she adds, "I see that now. I've been so selfish."

Naomi takes a breath. "I'm glad you can see where you might have been insensitive. That's good, that means you've snapped out of it. But it's not making an excuse to say that you were assaulted. Okay, maybe you were selfish to put yourself in that situation, but still. The only thing there's no excuse for is what that boy did to you. That's something you and Giannis should be supporting each other through, not fighting over. You've both been victims of it in your own ways."

"I haven't been supportive of him," Androulla says.

"So, start being. It's obviously not too late if he's still there," Naomi urges her.

Androulla bows her head and a raindrop slides off her hood. Despite Naomi's youth, she delivers her wisdom in an assured tone. The tone of someone who has begun their adult life with four years of university, an echo chamber of empowered voices. Unless she is going somewhere special, Naomi wears clothes that defy men to wonder what kind of body hides underneath. She is only bothered about their gazes when it suits her to be.

This attitude alarms and amazes Androulla, who won't leave the house if she doesn't feel thin or clear-skinned enough to be looked upon. By men. It is always men that she wants to like her, and women who she lets fall by the wayside. Perhaps because Oscar left. Perhaps because her father did, though she hates the idea that she is such a cliché. It is as possible that she isn't weak, just desperate to show that she relates to men more. She always has – probably because of her hormone imbalance – and must prove it with vulgar jokes and suggestive comments. Otherwise, she feels alone. She can't reference porn around her female friends without disgusting them. Nor, she fears, can she talk to the men she knows about feeling ravaged without disappointing them. They will think she is all talk, if she does. That she has been exaggerating her sex drive for years and is just like every other girl. Giannis might decide that she is less than him after all, in her physicality. Either that, or Androulla could keep letting him believe that she is more – too much. Somehow, neither narrative feels entirely true or false.

"I love him so much. I can't believe I hurt him like that and didn't even apologise. I want to make things right," Androulla says.

"Then you will," Naomi determines.

November

The Eleventh

"THERE SHE IS," GIANNIS grins, as Androulla steps up to the bar.

She has never seen him at work before and would think he was playing at it, with the tea towel hooked through his belt loop, if his cheeks weren't flustered red. The bar itself is twelve stools long, the establishment as a whole able to seat up to two-hundred people, Giannis has told her. He and just one other bartender are responsible for making the drinks.

"Androulla *mou*, this is Theo," he says.

Androulla brings her gaze down from the shelf of gin and whiskey bottles underlining the ceiling, past posters of seventies rock bands and retro beer signs, to see a man in a baseball cap.

"Theo, this is my wife. Androulla."

"Hey," Theo says.

Androulla keeps a level smile, even as Theo eyes her from under the brim of his cap. She has heard about him, how he trails off mid-sentence when a moderately good-looking woman walks past. She thought about this as she was getting dressed, and worried the sleeve of a tight-fitting top between her finger and thumb. Then she pulled on a sweatshirt. Dragging a stool out, she sits at the bar.

"Have a seat," Theo says, to Giannis. "I've got this."

"Are you sure?" Giannis asks.

Theo sweeps his hand along the bar, where one other group is clustered. Behind them, the knocks and clacks from a pool table inspire roars of frustration and joy. Otherwise, only a gentle murmuring pervades above the guitar-heavy music.

"It's one a.m. No one new is coming now," Theo says.

He sends Giannis yelping around the bar with a whip of his tea towel. Androulla reigns in her laughter when he flashes her a smile.

"Hi, Wife," Giannis greets her, softly.

She leans into the warmth of his kiss. "Hi, Wife . . ."

His t-shirt is thick with the smell of yeast, his breath ripe with alcohol. She pulls back.

"Your hair's wet," Giannis says, twirling a lock around his finger.

"Yeah, it was raining." She runs a hand back from her forehead.

"I'm glad you came," he says.

She smiles.

"Who do we have here?" a voice enquires, over her shoulder.

Androulla turns to greet three more of Giannis's colleagues. Imran, who has travelled from Pakistan to work and cannot go back even to visit. Mircea, who sends half her wages to her daughter in Romania. Abdou, who has come from Cameroon to study at American College.

"Nice to meet you all," Androulla says.

"And that's Iris."

At the sound of a door swinging open, Androulla turns. Emerging from the kitchen with her arms hanging by her sides is a girl with long, honeyed hair. She is taller than Androulla. Not skinnier per say but skinny in a nicer, less effortful way. The kind of thoughtless, painless skinny that only youth can make a girl, and yet her face is spotless. She is nineteen, Giannis has confessed.

"She's here from Thessaloniki, also studying," Abdou says.

Androulla looks back at him. "And what's your subject?" she asks.

As he tells her about his degree in Computer Science, a flicker registers between Imran and Mircea. It is gone when Androulla looks straight at them.

"Guys, do you want a drink?" Theo asks.

"I'll have a Keo," Giannis says, swinging his leg over the stool beside Androulla's.

"And for the lady?" Theo says.

"Erm." She looks to Giannis.

"We've got a zero-percent Carlsberg," he responds, in a low voice. "Or Coke, lemonade, anything like that."

"Okay," she says, looking back at Theo. "Could I have a Carlsberg, please? *Chorís alkoól.*"

Pulling Giannis's pint, Theo looks sideways at her. "Are you . . ?"

"No. Not pregnant," she says, with an apologetic smile.

The glimmer fades from his eyes as he releases the beer tap. "I'm sober."

Giannis's beer hits the bar with a thud. He twitches, but rests a supportive hand on Androulla's back. She leans into it while Theo walks the length of the bar to fetch her drink. She discovered within days of declaring herself off-alcohol that people would not accept this. Even her parents and grandparents couldn't fathom it. Just have one, people urged her, once they had established that she was not pregnant. Her stomach feels hollow.

When she says that she is sober, no one pushes her. They assume that Androulla has suffered a long and terrible battle with alcohol. And she feels like she has, in a way. In the summer, she drank more than she had in all her life before. At first this was to buoy her spirits with Giannis away. Then it was to bolster her confidence for the open mic nights where Pantelis took her, to hear his poems and meet his friends. By the time Naomi came to stay, Androulla was reeling around as though at the end of a lawless night out. Dissociation felt disconcertingly similar to a certain pitch of drunkenness, and the fact that she had been pushing through both states on an empty stomach for months had done her no favours. She looks horribly thin and wild-eyed in their photos, she sees now.

Androulla tugs her hands into her sleeves. She didn't feel thin at the time. She didn't see how far off-centre she was, that the amount of porn she was watching with her husband away was warping her perception, getting her used to and expectant of things that were not normal. It was terrifying, the echo chamber that she and Giannis had created for themselves over the phone, like it was a long and hard-walled tunnel they were calling through. You can convince yourself that anything is acceptable, if you are exposed to enough of it and have just one other person agreeing with you, Androulla has realised. When she was in that state, constantly drunk or hungover, simultaneously sex-starved and sex-crazed, questioning her womanhood and vying to either prove or disprove it once and for all, she thought society had got it all wrong. They had figured it out, her and Giannis and no one else. Institutions like monogamy were archaic and should be challenged. The assumption of children was ignorant and vapid. Selfish, actually, with the state of the world.

Theo places a bottle down in front of her. "Do you want a glass?"

Androulla stops her nose halfway to wrinkling. "Actually, yeah. Thank you," she smiles.

The bar feels sticky beneath her hands.

"Are you okay?" Giannis asks her, quietly.

"Mmn hmn," she says.

"Are you sure?" He is looking deep into her eyes, poised for a sign of discomfort. At her nod, he sits back. "It's very impressive, you know. What you're doing," he signals, with a nod at her drink. "I couldn't do it."

"Well, I know that," she says, angling her glass under the bottle.

Giannis returns her grin. "Christ, alright," he says, taking a swig of his pint.

It leaves a line of white foam over his lip and they laugh.

The kitchen door swings open, emitting a manager who cuts through the room with his palms pressed together at his forehead.

"That's his shark fin," Theo explains, as the runners scatter from the bar. "He wants to keep the staff circulating, so he gives them all the same spiel when they join. Apparently, if a shark stops moving, it'll die."

"Right," Androulla says.

At his shrug, she launches into a harder laugh than either he or Giannis does, and covers it with her glass. It is easy enough to affect a 'pub laugh', as she has taken to thinking of it, but harder to gage the right moment. How drunk her company is, how sorely her sobriety will stick out if she fails to match their reactions to things.

"This isn't bad," she says, swallowing the cold liquid.

Giannis is slow to respond. Androulla looks to where his head was just turned, and tightens her grip on her glass. At the far end of the bar, Iris is tapping at a till screen with manicured fingernails. She has a finer nose and lips than Androulla does, and lighter eyes and hair. Thessaloniki is a more north-western part of Greece than Rhodes, where Androulla's mother is from. Androulla has always been grateful of the dark features that she inherited from Olympia, especially since she has aspired to her stepfather and his Cypriotness. But perhaps Giannis likes paler girls.

He gives an overeager nod, pointing Androulla back to her drink. "You like that one, do you? Is it convincing?" he asks.

She is opening her mouth to answer when Theo shouts down the bar.

"Iris," he says, holding out a short drink. "I messed this one up earlier."

"What was it meant to be?" Iris asks, as a ticket curls from the till.

"A Negroni," Theo says. "Gin, Campari, sweet vermouth."

With a smirk, Iris plucks the ticket free. "And what did you do to it?"

"Doubled the Campari," Theo grins.

To hoots of delight from her colleagues, Iris downs the drink in one. Her Greek sounds 'clean'. Perhaps sophisticated, where Androulla would have said pretentious. Her manner is dirty. Or 'fun', in a way that Androulla has found to be dangerous.

"I'll be back in a minute," she mumbles, climbing off her stool.

"Are you okay?" Giannis frets, reaching after her.

Imran offers him nachos at the same time as Androulla says that she is just going to the toilet. He will figure it out, she decides, as the door thumps shut behind her. A relief. The music sounds distant, like it is floating down to Androulla at the base of a well. She leans against the tiled wall, with the sound of the rain dripping down through an open window, and pulls out her phone. On the home screen are two new apps, Alcoholics Anonymous and Sex Addicts Anonymous, neither of which she has opened much since she discovered their religious leanings. But it is nice to know they are there, their icons like chips that she has already earned, keeping her going.

If Imran brings out a plate of nachos, it will be okay that Androulla doesn't have any because she has eaten dinner. And breakfast and lunch, a spinach smoothie and a berry smoothie. She is trying to have those every day now, with snacks of nuts or vegetables and a whole dinner in the evening. For the first time in months she has been running, too, depleting her body and satisfying her mind that she is burning energy. She must restore it, to stop that lightheaded feeling. She doesn't want to come untethered from her body again.

'Hey,' she texts Naomi, 'sorry I missed you earlier. How did the interview go? Xx'.

'Really well!' Naomi replies, instantly. 'They asked literally every question you said they would, so weird'. She adds, 'Thank you for practising with me xx'.

Pride swells in Androulla's chest. She can still remember how fragile Naomi was the first time she stepped into a therapy room, how small and frightened of the world after the tragedy it had inflicted upon her. In eleven years, she has grown into an assured woman, poised to help other young people. To hold her hand through so much of that growth, Androulla realises, has been the most fulfilling thing in the world. It doesn't matter that they are not blood-related.

'You deserve everything xxx', she writes back.

As she is turning to leave the toilets, the door swings inwards.

"Oh," Iris starts. The apology freezes upon her lips.

It is hard not to wonder how it felt for Giannis to kiss them, or whether at nineteen, Iris's skin was palpably younger than Androulla's is at twenty-four. It has never occurred to Androulla to be worried about her age. And she isn't, she decides, as Iris struggles, visibly, with whether to barge in or step aside. What Androulla has with her husband is more mature than that. They have moved beyond it. She twists sideways to let the girl pass and returns to the bar.

"Nachos," she says, brightly.

With a nervous look, Giannis pushes the plate towards her. "Do you want some?"

"I'm okay," she says, settling back onto her stool, "but thank you." She kisses him.

Clocking off, Abdou and Mircea sit down. Androulla greets them with broad smiles and gives Giannis's hand a squeeze, the dripping of the rain forgotten.

The Thirteenth

"Do you have your passport?" Kostas asks, as he brings the car to a stop.

"Yes," Androulla confirms, lifting up the side of her tote bag.

"Last year's visa card?"

She unclasps her wallet. "Mmn hmn."

Slowly, Kostas withdraws his keys from the engine.

"Do we need anything else?" Androulla asks.

With a shrug, he unclicks his seatbelt. "We'll find out, I guess."

With their previous trips here emblazoned upon her brain, Androulla is expecting the heat of summer when she opens her door. Instead, a light breeze blows up dust from the unpaved car park of Omonoia FC. Androulla feels almost cool with her arms bare, ducking beneath the branches of a pomegranate tree.

"It looks like rain," she says, craning past the fruit to see the sky streaked with clouds.

The car thuds to a lock.

As she follows her stepfather up the hill between fledgling apartment buildings, her French plaits weigh upon her shoulders. There is a drift of cigarette smoke and a pause in the clunking of metal against metal as a builder watches them pass. Androulla picks up her pace. Boys in sweats, speaking languages that she has come to recognise as Urdu and Arabic, sit in groups upon the walls of flower beds. Perhaps they are the boys from last year, back for renewal like Androulla. Except that she can't recall seeing anyone with their skin tones inside. All the characters whose cases she overheard when, at last, she made it into the Perspex-divided room with the air conditioning blasting in vain, were white. Lots of them wives from Russia. Some refugees from Ukraine. A few aged second-homeowners from England. With her mother's Greek tan, Androulla was the darkest among them. She follows her stepfather around a corner.

Immigration is an opaque glass box whose front door opens outwards.

"Excuse me," Kostas calls, before a security officer slams it shut.

"You have to go around the back," another voice sounds.

Androulla turns to see a young Cypriot woman. Unencumbered by a bag, she is waving them around the building with her passport in hand. Brand new, by the shine of its cover. Androulla supresses her urge to snatch it.

"Come on," her stepfather nudges her, thanking the woman.

They follow her directions, off the main road and down the side of the building. At the end of a concrete funnel, they are faced with a wall of metal bars twice their height. Security officers mumble into walkie-talkies on the other side, shaking their heads and ordering people back for their crying and shouting and invalid, vital matters. Some have lowered their eyes and packed themselves in under a metal sheet, the only shelter there was from the scorching heat of last summer. Androulla wonders if she will have to compete for a space beneath it today, glancing again at the sky. Her stepfather pushes her through the crowd.

"*Kaliméra sas*," he greets an officer, in 'clean' Greek.

The man gives a terse nod through the bars.

"We're here to renew my daughter's visa. She's currently here on 'extended stay' as my dependant," Kostas starts.

A crease appears between the officer's hazel eyes. "Your daughter," he repeats. "Doesn't she have a passport?"

Kostas opens and closes his mouth. "Well, she was my stepdaughter. I just adopted her," he explains, with one of his nervous laughs.

The officer is lighting a cigarette. As it catches, he gives another, singular jerk of his head.

"Her visa is running out in one month," Kostas goes on, signalling to Androulla.

She fumbles through her bag, elbowing one man and stepping on another's toe as she turns to apologise.

"Androulla *mou*," Kostas hurries her.

"Sorry," Androulla says, a third time. Her face burns as she holds up the card with her wide-stretched photo on it.

With his cigarette pinched to his lips, the officer nods. Amusement collects in his eyes before he turns back to Kostas and asks, through the strained end of an inhalation, "Do you have an appointment?"

"We do," Kostas says.

At his gesture, Androulla goes rummaging through her bag again, this time holding it close for the many pairs of darting eyes and shuffling feet around her. She finds the email on her phone. The security officer looks at it through the bars, then blows a flute of smoke out the side of his mouth.

"That's two weeks away," he says.

"We booked it a month earlier than we were advised to," Kostas says, "and she's still going to be late starting this process. *File mou*," he pleads, as the officer turns away.

His next exhalation streams into Androulla's eyes, making them water.

"What are we supposed to do if her time runs out? She has nowhere to go in England," her stepfather says, quietly.

"I can't let you in without an appointment," the officer maintains, looking past them.

"There are no appointments. Can you show him the website, Androulla *mou*?" Kostas persists, wrapping his hands around the bars. "They're all booked up for the next four months . . ."

Sticking his cigarette in his mouth, the officer takes hold of Androulla's phone. Her heart drops as he walks away with it, only calling back that he is going to show his colleague when he is several steps gone. He throws his cigarette to the tarmac and stops at a plastic table beneath the overhang of a one-storey car park.

Even now, half-caged and on the edge of deportation from the country that she has always called home, Androulla is fearful of seeing her phone in strangers' hands. They wouldn't have to scroll far through her photos to see the many naked pictures she took for Giannis while he was away. That wouldn't be very in keeping with her little-girl-in-need-of-looking-after act, would it? But it might help her case, she reminds herself. As though to prove this, a girl in black leggings and a low-cut top saunters up to the bars. She has dyed blonde hair, a full face of makeup and no appointment. Nonetheless, the gate screeches open and clanks shut behind her. Androulla can smell the girl's oversweet perfume long after she has clacked across the car park and into the building. Kostas is shaking his head when she looks at him.

"Unbelievable," he murmurs, his eyes fixed upon the responsible officer. "They're pigs."

Androulla's laugh comes out hollow. She resists her temptation to undo the topmost buttons of her shirt, an oversized short-sleeve that she is wearing in place of her tight dress from last year. She had made herself up to fit the pattern of girls getting through the gate, in too much makeup and little clothing, and it had worked. Her laughter had been full then, both disbelieving and delighted. Kostas had lowered his eyes, hurt that this was what it took for his country to accept his child.

"Who cares? We're in," Androulla had said, as they entered the building.

She was glowing with her success and, privately, with the smugness of feeling men's eyes on her back.

Now, her lip curls at the officer who let the blonde girl through, just so that he could watch her walk away. Perhaps the girl has also been here before and came dressed to play the men. Perhaps that is an empowering choice, Androulla thinks. But only because the circumstances dictate that it has to be.

At a knock to her elbow, she turns back to the bars.

"Oh. Thank you," she says, taking her phone from the hazel-eyed officer.

She searches his face for a sign that he has seen her photos, but there is none.

"Who's handling your case?" the officer asks.

"*Kyría* Xenofontos," Androulla answers.

Recognising this name, the officer nods. "If you can get her on the phone, you can go inside."

Androulla and Kostas call out their thanks as he walks away, then look at each other with wary eyes. It was Ms Xenofontos' unresponsiveness that pushed them up to the wire last year. In the three months before Androulla's tourist visa ran out, they had scrambled to get the relevant papers together, massaging what they had to, and then begged at her subordinates' desks. They had sent the department head everything required, tried calling at all times of day and left her voicemails. Androulla was facing deportation and, subsequently, homelessness. Ms

Xenofontos' subordinates said patient things with dull eyes, for they saw cases like Androulla's every day. Ms Xenofontos didn't pick up even when they called her direct line.

It was only by luck that she strayed downstairs in Androulla's final week, a middle-aged woman in a floral blouse. Having overheard Kostas's loudening pleas, she leaned over her subordinate's shoulder and introduced herself. Androulla blinked. This was Ms Xenofontos. This mild woman, flipping through the file that Androulla had done all but bleed to get in front of her, did not match the image she'd had in mind. Over *soúvla* at her grandparents', she had told stories of the Wicked Witch of Immigration, whose evil plan was to keep applicants waiting until their time in Cyprus ran out, rather than granting anyone status. Androulla almost despised the woman for saying that their paperwork looked fine and reading out her email address. When she confirmed that this was the address she had been using for months, Ms Xenofontos frowned. She approved Androulla's application that same day.

"She's not going to pick up," Androulla says, entering the number.

"Try," her stepfather urges her.

Stepping back from the bars to make way for newcomers, she lifts her phone to her ear. It rings out.

"No answer," she confirms.

"Try again," Kostas says.

As Androulla is going to redial, a drop of water lands on her screen. Wiping it off, she squints upwards. The rain is falling just hard enough to inspire a mass migration to the metal shelter. Taking a sideways step with everyone else, Androulla feels the humidity between bodies. This is what the authorities are afraid of. She wishes the weather wouldn't make such an example of them all, crowding into too small a space. As she calls Ms Xenofontos's office a second time, her gaze falls upon a child. He cannot be older than four or five, dark-skinned and crouched down, poking at something in the dirt. The woman who she presumes to be his mother gazes, listlessly, over his head. Androulla wonders how long they have been waiting. Many of those around her are black, and many more are of South Asian descent. To stand at the bars like this feels surreal. Like a scene from the world news, not from anyone's real life. Again, the phone rings out in Androulla's ear.

"There must be another way," she says, lowering it.

"She didn't answer?" Kostas asks.

When Androulla says no, he shakes his head at the hazel-eyed officer and leads her back around the building.

"So that's it? We're giving up?" she calls, after him.

The windscreen wipers wave from passing cars.

"We'll go back in two weeks. Unless you can get Xenofontos on the phone before then," Kostas says.

"You know that's not going to happen." Androulla opens her car door into a dangling pomegranate and watches it rock through her window. "How can it be this difficult? You've adopted me," she says, as Kostas climbs in beside her.

"And if you were under twenty-one, you would have got your passport automatically. But . . ." He gives a weary shrug.

"I grew up with this culture as much as any Anglo-Cypriot, and they all get passports," Androulla argues. "Just because we're not blood-related . . . It should be the same," she says.

It has to be the same. Otherwise, what kind of absolvent can it be of an absent father? What kind of solution to the inability to conceive a child? The rain comes harder at Androulla's window.

"I'm sorry, Androulla *mou*," Kostas says, for the first time raising his voice. "What did you expect? This is immigration. I have friends who went to the U.S. eleven years ago and they're still trying to get their status. You know, you come from England . . ."

"I grew up in England," she corrects him.

"Grew up in England, okay," he says, spreading his hands. "So your understanding of what it takes to get accepted into a different country has been sheltered. Hasn't it changed already, since we've been here?" he asks.

"It's changed since Brexit," she mutters.

"Even without being in the EU, though, you have some advantage," Kostas says.

She turns her scowl upon him.

"You may not feel like you do," he says, "but think about what just happened. Did you see that guard arguing with anyone else, any of the people from the Philippines or the Congo, for as long as he argued with us?"

Androulla stares at him.

"I know how much Cyprus means to you, I understand your frustration. This is a hard, hard process," Kostas concludes. "But it could be harder." He turns his key in the ignition.

Androulla sits in silence as they pull away from the pomegranate tree. The fruit stops its swinging, just as the windscreen wipers squeak into motion.

The Nineteenth

Giannis's eyes move side to side down the laptop screen. He scrolls fluidly as he reads, his fingers curled at a fond angle to the touchpad. Androulla watches him until she cannot stand to any longer, then gets up from the table. She leaves behind the book that she has been staring over, one by a Greek author that Pantelis recommended. It is enjoyable but dense, and hard to focus on when she is hyperaware that someone is reading her book, simultaneously. She has shared snippets with her husband along the way, and he has read all her previous works. But this one is different. She can feel its words quivering under his gaze, as if they have remained shifting, changing parts of her even since she committed them to the document.

When she reaches the doorway, she stops. It is nine p.m. She could offer Giannis a drink, but she doesn't want to break his concentration. He sighs.

"Are you okay? Bored?" she frets, looking back at him.

"Just breathing," he murmurs, his eyes fixed to the screen.

Androulla posts herself at the kitchen sink, water glass in hand. The smell of paprika hangs in the air from their rice-and-beans dinner. Tonight, a Spanish rendition. A steady rain is coming down beyond the window, giving the city an eerie glow. Despite the darkness, Androulla's vision is clear. She can identify the Wargaming headquarters, the 360 apartment building on Makarios Avenue, and the Pentadaktylos Mountains by their blue, red and gold-flashing lights alone. The water slips cool down her throat.

"Okay, Wife," Giannis calls.

Androulla turns on her heel. Her husband is leaning back in his chair when she re-enters the living room, with his arms stretched overhead. He reaches them towards her.

"Did you finish it?" she asks, as she approaches him.

"Yeah," he says, returning to the touchpad as though to make sure.

She stops. "And? What did you think?"

A grin spreads across his face. "I think I married a genius."

"Stop," she laughs, continuing towards him. But she has to ask, "Really?"

He hugs her around the waist, kissing up the side of her torso. "This is amazing. It feels . . ." He pulls his head back. "I don't mean to insult to anything you're written before, but this one reads like a real book. Is that fair to say? Do you think . . ?"

"Yeah, I think so too," Androulla assures him. She disentangles herself from his arms, gripped with talking about it. "So, what made you think that? Was there anything in particular that felt different this time?"

Giannis looks back at the screen. "The characters were well-rounded. Everyone was clearly defined from the beginning, and they'd all grown by the end," he says.

Androulla feels herself nodding, eagerly. She shifts her weight onto her back foot. "What about the ending? Did you think it made sense for Ariadne?"

"Yeah?" Giannis says, lacing his hands behind his head. "I mean, she isn't the most riveting character. You know, young girl from a middle-class background. I won't say I was too invested in what happened to her because whatever it was, ultimately, I knew she'd be alright. It was the surrounding characters I was in it for."

"Yes! That's the point, that's exactly what I wanted!" Androulla cries, clapping her hands. She clasps them together as she explains, "My idea was to weave a kind of tapestry of the different lives we'd seen intersecting since we moved here. Because Cyprus is, you know . . ."

"Oh, it's a clusterfuck," Giannis says.

"I was going to say melting pot, but yeah." Androulla smiles. "What I really wanted to focus on was, like, the changeable nature of privilege. And how it's relative, depending on where you are, to your race and religion and class." She tucks her hair behind her ears. "Did that come across?"

Giannis lowers his hands to nod.

"And you don't think it was cancellable, the way I wrote about people from other backgrounds?" Androulla asks.

He frowns. "What about it would be cancellable?"

"I don't know. Even, just, where I've described different skin tones . . ." She bites her lip.

Shaking his head, Giannis reminds her, "It's not offensive to give a visual, especially if it's relevant to what you're writing about. These are important issues. Plus, what's the alternative? Shying away from characters with different backgrounds? Then you'd be excluding them."

"Yeah," Androulla supposes.

"The message is good," Giannis assures her. "You're clearly in favour of peace and love all around. And you haven't given any 'opinions' along the way, you've just made observations. Of things you've actually seen," he adds.

She releases her lip. "That's true. So, you like it?"

"I love it," he says, reaching his arms around her again. "And I think publishers will too."

"Do you now," she laughs, into his hair.

Pressing her lips to his head, she inhales his familiar scent, faintly mixed with cigarette smoke from his day shift at the bar.

With his temple resting against her ribcage, Giannis gazes up at her. "This could change everything. I'm serious," he says, when she pulls away. "Imagine if you got a publishing deal in the UK. If you made enough money, we could just buy our way in here like the Russians do. Get a property and get residency. No more insecurity, we'd have our future settled . . ."

Relief washes through Androulla. To hear Giannis talking about a future with her again, after the months they have had, makes her hold him closer.

"I'll try," she says, setting her sights on the last line of her sixty-thousand word document, "if you believe in me."

"I've always believed in you," he says.

"I know. I'd probably have given up years ago, if you hadn't," she admits.

"I don't think so." Giannis reaches a palm up to her heart. "It's in you to write. You'd always have found a way," he says.

She smiles. Twisting his head around, Giannis buries his face in the flat of her stomach and kisses it. The warmth where his palm was fades.

"I've been meaning to talk to you, on the subject of security," Androulla says, "about adoption."

The screen of her laptop goes dark.

"Okay," Giannis blinks.

She stands back from him. "I haven't been thinking about the kid thing. But I've been thinking about, thinking about it," she says. "Just because, with my condition, we should probably know what our options are. In case we do change our minds . . ." She trails off, digging her thumbnail into the skin of her pinkie.

Giannis lets out a long breath. "Makes sense. That's why I've been looking into it," he says.

Androulla's heart skips. "You've been looking into adoption?" she repeats.

"While I was back in Australia, I was. Before . . ." He gives a sideways motion with his head.

"Oh," she says, releasing her hands.

A breeze casts the rain at the window, then drops away.

"I'd start looking again. Not for now, obviously," he says. "But for the future, maybe."

A breath of wonder escapes Androulla. "Any other surprises?"

Giannis shrugs. "I also wrote something, for the first time in a while."

"A new poem?" she asks, taking the seat opposite him.

"Kind of." His smile slides into a grimace. "It's more a stream-of-consciousness, automatic type thing."

She pushes her laptop shut between them. "Will you read it to me?"

"Now?"

She nods.

Shifting forwards, Giannis pulls his phone from his trouser pocket. "Okay," he says, as his eyes take on the sheen of its brightness. He clears his throat. "'Roads. Evoking the veins of the urban through which your life runs, alongside faceless bodies and wandering minds. Joined at the heart by coincidence'," he reads, in a low voice. Then looks up. "I haven't been over this by the way, so if it's cringey . . ."

"Keep going," Androulla urges him.

He takes a breath. "'Thin, tanned fingers depressing the keys of a laptop and the lingering smell of tobacco. Melbourne. London. Nicosia. Wide white rooms, lit well in early summer. Time to leave, you think, and you can see her naked body draped across the bed in the honey of the sun. You never asked for this. Any of it, you think. The door handle is made of brass and so warm in your palm. It catches as it twists, like a dislocating shoulder. Fourteen paces into the street and the first drop of sweat weighs your shirt down. Why are you in Cyprus? Why aren't you? Where did you find her? With the hair like flannel and the skin like bed sheets. In the street, women chat and men don't. There are motorbikes and a sense that things are moving, pulsing around the veins of the city. And then you stop. Maybe that makes you cholesterol. Catch a train in your hands like a tennis ball. Bounce it up and down while sitting in your grandmother's yard, smelling the pink roses before they were gone. The sky is still blue though. No, her skin wasn't like bed sheets, it was like paper. Blank parchment, and you never had the right quill. And maybe when summer comes to the Southbank once more and the electric sky glints against the flashing pavements, or even in autumn when the ribbons of rain drain the faceless from the streets, maybe, maybe, maybe, you'll catch another train. Maybe you will board that one with fewer suitcases. Ensconced in thin metallic comfort, you faced against the direction of travel and it took you anyway. No, not paper'," Giannis concludes. "'Paper tears underwater.'"

He lowers his phone. Androulla opens her mouth, but there is only the sound of the rain coming down beyond the window.

Worry blooms in her husband's eyes as the tears spill from hers. She stands.

"I'm sorry," he murmurs, wiping her cheek. Then his.

She shakes her head, climbs onto his lap. And they hold each other, quietly, for a long time.

The Twenty-Second

It is like a shadow, her relationship with her father. A photo negative. The cuttings left over from around a stencil drawing, in that he never sees the whole picture. Androulla can recall being ten years old and trying to tell him, as he drove her to his house one Friday night, that she felt like he didn't know who she was. She didn't have the perspective or the vocabulary to explain what she meant then, about how tense she was around him, so desperate to impress that she felt contrived. And it still wasn't good enough. He never saw her with her friends, what they were like or how they interacted. She was welcome to invite them over, he said, and Androulla felt her bottom lip grow large. Weren't their weekends together as precious to him as they were to her? Didn't the weeks between them stretch longer every time he checked his calendar? Androulla couldn't invite her friends to take up that time. It meant too much to her, and too little to her father. Always.

She understood from an early age that she was obsessed with him. That when he was listening to a new album and his brow furrowed, the music turned flat in her ears. When they sat side by side watching a panel show and his shoulders shook, she laughed, too. Not because she had followed the joke, but because she wanted to be in on whatever was amusing her father so much. To this day, her favourite film is one that Giannis doesn't understand the merit of. A cult classic, Gary used to say. They might only have watched it together twice, but Androulla can quote all the best lines. 'As you wish.' 'You killed my father, prepare to die.' 'Inconceivable!' She loves it. But she also knows that she would never have watched a film like that, parodying the adventures of pirates and princesses, of her own accord.

Perhaps her father is one of the 'shiny' people, as Olympia refers to them. As a child, Androulla brought home so much upset from her shiny classmates that her mother had to warn her about them, sternly. There were some people, she explained, who had a lure, a pull. A shine. Everyone clamoured to get close to them. But when the shine wore off, they were mean and would drop the 'best friend' in their entourage overnight. It took Androulla two or three experiences like this to understand. And to wonder if her mother had found out about the shiny people from Gary, when he swept her so violently off her feet that she forgot her home country in ten days, only to face her subsequent pregnancy alone. It is possible. Everyone who meets Gary, in a limited capacity, seems enamoured with him. He is quick-witted and politically sound by London standards, yet outrageous enough with the odd comment. Like a breeze blowing up someone's skirt and making them shriek with laughter, even as they try to pin it down. He knows what to say and when. Unless he is talking to his daughter.

His thoughtlessness affected Androulla as she grew older. She took refuge in his house when her mother's throat turned hoarse with shouting, and noticed then the very English lump in his, the fact that he would sooner swallow than express any feelings. When Oscar said that he might be gay, a day after Androulla had curled her hand around him, she told her father that she was heartbroken. He said he was laughing because she was too young to know what she was talking about. Then Oscar died. Gary touched Androulla's shoulder, with a look upon his face that almost conceded some wrongdoing. But he kept belittling the things she said.

"I'm Cypriot."

"No, you're not," he sneered.

Androulla frowned. "Yes, I am." It was fact.

She gazes out her living room window at the rain coming down upon flat-roofed buildings, the water tanks crouching on steel legs, the pine trees stretching skywards from her local park. Everything that she has ever wanted a view of, but for the weather. Gary can accept that she is half-Greek because her mother is from Rhodes, and because she grew up speaking the language and reading the myths. Why, then, does he not count the 'c-h' sounds of the Cypriot dialect, or the various origin stories of the Five Finger Mountains that Androulla also grew up with? She watches a raindrop trail down her window.

There is something about Cyprus that gets under the skin. It possesses you, compels you back with an arcane force. You cannot attribute its power solely to the clear waters, the staggering mountains or the spirited people, the sweet wine, the smell of *kléftiko* roasting on a Sunday or the fact that it rains only thirty-eight days a year. Despite their loveliness, the sum total of those elements would not be enough for Androulla and Giannis to drag themselves through the immigration process. For them to stunt their careers and accumulate debts, live hand-to-mouth and work overtime, fearing the law, there must be something more to it. An invisible current that runs with the rivers from Troodos into their hearts – never mind their veins – and which drives them to choose home over ease every time they are faced with another end date to one of their visas. Another restriction on what they can do with those visas. Another person like Androulla's father, who should know better, asking why the hell they are putting themselves through it. The raindrop slides down, out of sight.

Perhaps Androulla is being unfair. Perhaps the consequences of Gary's leaving have hurt him, too. After all, to let Androulla call herself Cypriot would be to admit that Kostas had been not only the man in her mother's life, or a cardboard cut-out in the corner of the room, but a living, breathing father figure with ideas and influence. In order for Gary to deny that to himself, he had to insist that Androulla was English. Somewhat Greek if she must be, but White British predominantly. It didn't matter that she took leftover vine leaves stuffed with mincemeat to school while her classmates packed ham sandwiches. The blood in her veins was Gary's.

At home, Androulla learned that this did not matter. It could not matter, because if Kostas couldn't call her his daughter then he would have to accept never being a parent, after Olympia's ectopic pregnancy. The notion was painful. Kostas would have made a wonderful father. And he did, Androulla feels, in all the ways that mattered. Sliding open the door to her window box balcony, she inhales the fresh smell of the rain.

Ultimately, it was Cyprus that came between her and her father. She doesn't think he would understand if she explained this to him, but by denying her Cypriotness he was dismissing an integral part of her. By continuing a relationship with him, she was reducing her claim to that part. And so it was easy, when he sniffed at the idea of her dating a Cypriot, to cut him off. Androulla had felt more passionately about her connection to Cyprus the longer that she had lived elsewhere. Like many members of the diaspora, she had stuck closer to the traditions of her motherland than anyone living there. Until she announced her move to Nicosia, and Gary didn't call her for two years. Androulla takes a shaky breath.

"Hello," she greets him, lifting her phone to her ear. "How are you?" Instead of her stepfather's signature 'where' are you.

"Yeah. Not bad, thanks," Gary says. "Are you alright?"

"I'm good. Thanks," Androulla adds.

She can hear the rain clearly with her balcony door open, coming down from a white sky.

"Have you been up to much this week?" her father asks.

More trips to Immigration flash across her mind. The paper declaring her Androulla Demetriou, not Androulla Dixon, sliding under a Perspex screen. The wedding ring missing from her finger as she pretended not to be married to Giannis, though she wasn't married to Giannis. Another relationship defined by how its members feel about it, rather than what it is.

"Not really. I've just been working," Androulla says.

She holds her palm out to feel the rain, but the balcony above hers blocks it. She falls back a step. She wants to tell her father she is frightened, that nothing in her life is going as planned. She has resorted to things that she never could have imagined before this year, for the difficulty of it. With her heels on the backs of her trainers, she steps outside. The wind whips up her hair and she holds her phone closer. More than anything, she wants to confess that she is excited. In the face of so much adversity, she has determined to turn things around. She has overhauled her diet, reintroduced exercise, worked on herself and her relationship in more profound ways than she had known were possible, written a book and sent it to agents. She has glimpsed some light, albeit at the end of a long tunnel. But it still feels strange, opening up to her father. They have only just started talking again.

"How about you?" she asks him. "Have you been busy?"

"I watched a good film last night," he says.

From the edge of her balcony, the rain lands cool on Androulla's palm. She no longer resents her father for sharing her blood. Nor does she fret about her closeness to Kostas, since she has read up on the separate-but-equal places for both biological and adoptive parents.

"Cool," she says, lowering her hand. "What was it?"

THE THIRTIETH

LIGHTNING SPARKS, STARTLING THE window sheet-white. Androulla sits tense upon her sofa until the thunder follows, hungry for more.

"That sounded closer," she says, looking up from her laptop.

"It's okay." Giannis gives her knee a squeeze. "Keep going."

It is after two a.m. and he has come home from work with the smells of malt and sweat. Just in time, by the pounding of the rain. Androulla has already been to sleep and woken up again. She is lying against one arm of the sofa with her legs draped over her husband's and her laptop balanced on top of them.

"Okay." She shifts to stop the sofa arm from digging into her back. "How's this for a response . . . 'Dear Peter, I hope you're well. Thank you for getting back to me so quickly. Please find attached the synopsis and first three chapters of my novel, as requested.'"

The window shocks white again. Androulla flinches, then gasps at a touch to her inner thigh. As the thunder rumbles, she looks at her husband's bright eyes and the suggestive twist of his lips. She lets him slide his hand further, then knocks it back with the base of her laptop.

"Carry on," he grins.

Androulla returns to her email. "'Once again, I'd like to thank you for your interest in my work. This story means a lot to me and to see it out in the world, touching other lives, would be truly . . .'"

Giannis withdraws his hand.

Another flash. As the thunder bellows after it, Androulla tilts her screen down.

"What?" she asks.

"Nothing," Giannis decides, leaning back against the sofa. "Finish reading it first."

"What is it?" she persists. "Did I say something wrong?"

"You didn't say anything wrong. It's just . . ." He sighs. "You're starting to grovel, and you don't need to do that. You already did in the first email, when you asked if he was interested."

Androulla wrinkles her nose. "Of course I did," she says. "These people have all the power. There's no getting published without an agent."

"Maybe they have the power, but you have the product," Giannis points out. "And they don't make any money if they're not selling products, do they? They want to like this book as much as you want them to like it," he assures her.

"But they must get so many submissions," Androulla says, pushing her screen back.

"So, stand out. Don't do all the bootlicking that everyone else probably does. Just say a simple thank you and move on."

Androulla gazes at her pleas, thinly veiled in thanks. All her hopes pinned to the attachments at the top of her email. Slowly, she brings the pad of her forefinger down on the backspace key and watches it steam, train-like, through her final paragraph. Again, the window lights up and her heart shrinks inwards.

"You'll be the one with the power soon," Giannis murmurs, under the roaring thunder. "When this book sells its first million copies, you'll be the one turning people away."

Androulla laughs. He is sliding his hand up her thigh again, this time stretching his fingers to ignite something between her legs. She shuts her laptop, cursor blinking. It lands unsteadily on the hard-tiled floor and she twists her head after it. Giannis is already leaning over her, pinning her hips in place. Androulla parts her lips to let in his tongue, as if to taste the world he speaks of. A world without borders, where her right to pull close to her husband – on her sofa in her home – isn't up for debate. She claws at his back as he touches her, then rolls down onto her knees and holds his gaze, bleary-eyed, until he tips his head back.

Lightning strikes, at one with the thunder that roils around them.

"Let's go to bed," Androulla says, as their reflection appears on the un-shuttered window.

She takes Giannis by the wrist into their room where the blinds are down, the bed unmade. He lingers between her legs while she lies back and closes her eyes. The rain is coming down hard, drumming a steady rhythm until the wind casts it against the window, startling Androulla upright. Giannis smirks, pleased with his work. She turns away from him. A short breath out and his lips are warming her shoulder, Androulla arching her back. In the thunder, she hears waves crashing on the distant shore as she hugged a stranger's neck, moments before he wrapped his hands around hers. In her ear, her husband's promises like the sea through a shell that she has been asking, since she was a child, whether Cyprus would love her back. Giannis's breaths turn hotter.

"Come inside," Androulla begs him, in a voice learned from Pornhub.

Lightning flashes between the blinds. As Giannis rolls off her, Androulla looks out. The thunder grumbles, some way from them now. The wind has dropped, leaving the rain to fall straight down upon the pavements. Androulla exhales.

"You embarrass me," Giannis says.

"And you me," she echoes, following him into the bathroom.

As he props up the toilet seat, she climbs around him into the shower. She ignores the black mould in the seam between wall and tray, and washes him out of her with cold water. She has been doing this for months, just in case. At first it was a precaution, a fearful 'just in case' the doctors were wrong.

"Do you think I'm pregnant?" she asked her husband, biting her lip.

He began by rolling his eyes, making her laugh. Then it became just another part of their post-coital ceremony, and Androulla stopped questioning it as she asked. The answer felt known, the measure of showering unnecessary.

"Just in case," she maintained, less with fear than with waning hope.

Putting the toilet seat down, Giannis turns to watch her through the glass. She still feels warm inside, with loose limbs from her release. They smile at each other, knowingly, before she turns off the shower. The sound of water coming down carries on beyond the window.

Reaching for her towel, Androulla asks, "Do you think I'm pregnant?"

Giannis's smile turns weary, then slips away. He shakes his head. "I just don't think that's going to happen, Androulla *mou*."

The towel comes rough to her skin.

She nods. "Yeah."

Miles away, the storm rumbles on.

December

The Ninth

It has been two weeks since Naomi began her training at CAMHS.

"What does that stand for again?" Androulla asks, resting her phone on the edge of her bathroom sink.

"Child and Adolescent Mental Health Services," Naomi's voice echoes, on loudspeaker. "Obviously didn't make much of an impact on you," she laughs.

Androulla sprays some glass cleaner onto a rag, turning it a darker yellow. "Maybe that's because they hadn't hired you yet," she coos.

"Oh, yeah. I would have been very useful around that time," Naomi retorts. "Nine years old with a recently deceased brother, who I had just watched my sister wank off."

Even as she laughs along, twelve years later, Androulla feels a tightness come into her jaw. "For the record, we were not sisters then," she says. "Let's try to keep a degree of separation between

Oscar as your brother and me as your sister when we tell that story, shall we? Please."

"Or, let's just never tell that story," Naomi says, the amusement drying up from her voice. "You haven't, have you?"

Androulla sets the bottle of glass cleaner down rocking. "What? Told anyone about me and Oscar . . ?"

"Us and Oscar," Naomi reminds her.

"Never," Androulla says, stilling the bottle. "Except Giannis. And a couple of the therapists I had after Oscar passed."

The chemicals rush up her nose.

"Why?" she asks. "You don't think anyone you're working with now might remember you from what I said, do you?"

"No!" Naomi cries. "I'm not broadcasting any details. Even if I was, I seriously doubt there's anyone from back then still working here."

"Probably not," Androulla agrees, lifting her rag to the mirror.

In her eight months at CAMHS, she had four therapists. She was tentative about opening up until the first one went on maternity leave, undiscouraged by the things she had heard from Androulla and other children. It was belittling, Androulla felt. And so she didn't hold back from telling Therapist Number Two about her night with Oscar before his death, which she had deemed too appalling for Therapist Number One. She didn't know another twelve year old girl who had done what she had. Whether or not it shocked Therapist Number Two, Androulla never knew. He was promoted within a few weeks. With a deep breath in, Androulla went over everything she had told him with Therapist Number Three, even detailing Naomi's presence in Oscar's bedroom that night. They formed a good bond. Androulla was making progress before the woman moved away. She faced Therapist Number Four with resignation. The thought of starting over, yet again, made her feel fatigued. That was when her parents made the stretch for some private sessions, which they couldn't sustain beyond three months.

"It is weird, being on the other side of it," Naomi says. "The one person in the world to know all someone's secrets."

"It's kind of cool," Androulla says, as she smears the glass cleaner in arcs over the mirror. "Especially with teenagers, just slagging off their parents and classmates, right? You love that kind of drama."

"I do," Naomi says, "but it's not like I can get the popcorn out in this situation. I'm not allowed to give my opinion, you know? So even the melodrama is kind of dry to talk about. And the other stuff . . ." She trails off.

Breath held, Androulla rubs hard at stubborn fleck of toothpaste. When it comes off, she says, "Hello?"

"Hi. Yeah, I'm here," Naomi responds.

"Oh. So you were saying, the other stuff. What other stuff?" Androulla prompts her.

Slowly, Naomi exhales. "Like, I'm realising now that this may sound naïve, I don't know. But I honestly thought I'd had the worst childhood because of Oscar."

"Of course," Androulla says.

"But it's nothing compared to . . ." Again, Naomi catches herself. "It's difficult, sorry. I can't give any specifics."

"That's okay," Androulla says, as her reflection peels into focus through the fading cleaning product. She lowers her rag to the sink.

"I think I may have underestimated how much it was going to affect me," her sister admits. "Sitting in that room all day, listening to one horror story after another. Maybe that sounds stupid as well."

"It doesn't."

"But I really believed I'd been through the worst, and done so many years of therapy myself that I was almost immune to trauma. It's a lot of pressure, having other people's put on you. And I'm not even in the room by myself yet, I'm shadowing."

"Well, that's good," Androulla says.

"Even the kids whose circumstances are less awful, though," Naomi persists. "You can see on their faces that they're reliving the worst things they, personally, have experienced. It doesn't matter if that's physical violence at home, or verbal abuse at school. They get this reflection in their eyes like a bomb's exploding over your shoulder, the first time they see that people are capable of hurting each other. This one boy looked really shaken up. I kept turning around but there was nothing there, obviously. His eyes were just darting."

Androulla picks up her phone.

"I thought that being able to relate to those feelings would make me good at this job, but what if it means I can't do it? It's too triggering? And I've just wasted four years and fifty grand on this degree . . ."

"You haven't wasted anything. Naomi, the support you've given me in these last few months has been enough to justify that already," Androulla says, turning her back to the mirror.

Naomi sniffs. "Thanks."

Taking shallows breaths of rubbing alcohol, Androulla wrenches open the window. A light drizzle is coming down outside, making the world feel both rotten and fresh.

"You think you're worth me being in all that debt then, do you?" her sister asks, with a hint of amusement.

"Absolutely," Androulla declares.

They share a laugh.

"I mean it, though. You've been amazing," she says. "I don't know where I'd have ended up without you, this summer."

"Stripping, maybe."

"Mmn. At the very least, divorced."

"Well . . ."

"You know what I mean."

Another, shorter laugh.

"I'm glad you felt like you could come to me," Naomi says. "But I don't know how to get that trust from people I've just met. There are techniques to do with body language and stuff, but those only work if a client is open to them."

"Yeah," Androulla says, turning her rag upon the shower panel.

"I saw this one girl, a sixteen-year-old, who'd bounced around between therapists for years. She'd done interpersonal, CBT, family therapy . . . When my supervisor introduced us, I smiled and she just gave me this look she couldn't stand me. Like she probably knew more than I did. And she's right, I've just graduated. How am I supposed to help her when people older and more qualified than I am have failed already?" Naomi asks.

"Maybe they failed because they couldn't understand her," Androulla says, spraying more glass cleaner across the panel. As it settles, filling the air with a scent like mouthwash, she stands back. "Did I ever tell you? I'm sure my last therapist used to laugh at the things I considered problems. She would just give me this look sometimes like, 'Really?' She never said it, obviously. My parents were paying her."

Naomi laughs.

"But because you're younger, you'll understand the issues facing this girl's generation," Androulla encourages her. "She'll see."

Naomi sighs. "I hope so. Plus, all jobs get easier over time, right? You hated working at that estate agent's in the beginning."

"Oh, from beginning to end," Androulla says.

She recalls the cramped office that smelled of her colleagues' microwave lunches, their snide jokes and the lettings contracts they had put her in charge of at nineteen. The six-day weeks of uploading new properties to Rightmove, only after she had 'blue-skied' the photos to make them look more appealing. Androulla can't believe how much of her job that constituted, in retrospect. Drawing her pointer around the edges of slate roofs and angular chimneys, then overlaying cloudless skies while her manager's eyes bored into her back and the pay remained awful. Androulla looks out her window and knows that today's rain is an anomaly.

Forgetting Giannis's fears that their electricity might be cut off, she says, "But it does get easier, yes."

Three-hundred and twenty-seven days a year, the sun shines.

"Thank you. I needed this," Naomi says. Then jibes, "Maybe you were worth the fifty grand to put right."

"Yeah," Androulla laughs. "Well, I'm glad to be back."

She buffs the shower panel clear.

The Twelfth

Returning to the coffee shop where she first met with Pantelis, Androulla takes a seat on the sheltered side of the courtyard. A green awning flaps above her, along with the bracts of a bougainvillea vine overhanging the adjacent wall. Only one other table is taken, by a woman wearing berry pink lipstick. She looks up from her phone and Androulla looks away. It took all her might to leave home with nothing but tinted sun cream on her face. Having risen early to meet a deadline, she logged off from work and watched her shoulders sag in the bathroom mirror. She had to put a face on, she thought. And caught herself. Why? If she didn't feel like it, then who was she doing it for? Not her husband, who was sleeping off a late shift at the bar and would later be going to UNic. That left Pantelis. In the months that she was 'allowed' to, Androulla had flirted with him. Had felt it was as important that he was attracted to her as it was that all men were attracted to her. But that was the kind of thing that she wasn't wearing makeup for anymore.

She stands up to greet the poet, and he envelops her in one of his padded embraces. He smells like clean laundry and cigarette smoke.

"You want to be outside, right?" she asks, as they draw apart.

"If that's okay." With a grimace, he takes a lighter and cigarettes from his coat pocket.

"Yeah, of course," Androulla says, dragging her chair out. Its steel legs screech.

"It's still not that cold yet. Although," she starts, squinting skywards. She is too fearful of sounding English to comment on the showers that have been falling, on and off.

"It's been a weird day weather-wise, right?" Pantelis smiles.

His car keys jingle as he sets them down upon the table. At the sight of them laid out – in an amnesty with his phone and sunglasses – Androulla smiles back. It confused her that Kostas 'declared' his valuables like this until she saw that in Cyprus, everyone seemed to. There was none of the whipping out and away of wallets that there was in England. Of course, Androulla's father was aghast when she brought this behaviour to a Pizza Express. She gave him her stepfather's explanation, that it was comfier not to have everything 'jamming in her pockets' when she sat down. But Gary didn't like her spreading herself over the table. She was a girl, he said, she could carry a bag. And put away her keys to his house before someone snatched them.

Pantelis tucks himself into the table. "So," he says, still gripping the sides of his chair. "You said you had some news?"

"Yes," Androulla says. She flattens her palms upon the cold tabletop.

"*Geiá sas*," the proprietor greets them, poised with his notebook.

Androulla orders her usual plain black coffee, Pantelis one with milk and sugar.

"*Efcharistó*," he thanks the proprietor, sitting back.

A breeze ruffles the courtyard's cherry tree, now bare of blossoms.

"I told you I was sending my book to agents in the UK," Androulla says.

Pantelis nods.

"So, I heard back from four of them within a week."

"Wow," he says, his eyes lighting up with the end of his cigarette.

"Not with yeses," she explains.

The lighter clunks as he places it down.

"But they were interested in what I'd written, and wanted some sample chapters and a synopsis."

"So, you sent those," he assumes, holding her gaze.

"I did." She slides her hands off the table. "And I got my first no back two days ago."

"Oh," Pantelis says, lowering his cigarette. "I'm sorry."

Androulla shrugs. "It's okay. I was probably naïve to think it would get picked up straight away. I did think that though," she admits, "because I'd written books before, and none of them had felt so fully formed as this one. So I went back and read over it myself."

Pantelis frowns. "To see why it was rejected, you mean?"

As her nod gives way to a headshake, Androulla covers her face. "Panteli . . ."

"That bad?" he laughs, tapping the ash off his cigarette. "Really? But you were so excited when you were writing it."

"I was," Androulla says, lowering her hands. "And I still think the story is good, or most of it is. It just has this ending to do with charity work," she explains, "which honestly, I threw in kind of at random because I didn't know what else to do . . . The whole idea was to have the protagonist be very bland, and just observe all these different situations with characters whose lives were more complicated than hers, because of their backgrounds or religious beliefs. I didn't want money to be an object for her, because I thought it would distract from those more important issues."

"Okay," Pantelis says.

Androulla tucks her hair back. "So obviously, this girl sees some stuff that really shocks her. And when I got to the end I was like, well, what am I going to do here? I can't have her witness these tragedies and just move on with her life, that would be awful. It should bother her enough that she wants to do something about it, right? Otherwise she'd seem heartless. But now that I've thought more about it . . ."

"*Oríste*," the proprietor says, returning with their coffees.

The cups rattle to stillness upon their saucers.

Thanking him again, Pantelis leans closer. "You were saying?"

"Just that, I'm afraid it might read kind of like a white saviour story?"

"And you think that's why the agent didn't take you?" he asks.

"I mean, I'm less worried about that," Androulla says.

Pantelis tilts his head.

"This is going to sound like a 'snowflakey' term, but I've been thinking about unconscious bias."

He takes a drag on his cigarette.

"When I started the book," she explains, "I was writing from a place of feeling 'other' in England. Even though I grew up there, I never considered myself White British because I was raised in a house with different cultures. I saw my parents get stigmatised, my stepfather attacked. And so I think, because of that, I felt entitled to write from the perspective of a character that sympathised with people from less fortunate backgrounds. I didn't see it as condescending."

"That makes sense," Pantelis says, turning his head to exhale.

"But living here," Androulla says, "I feel the whitest I ever have. Like, despite everything with Immigration," she goes on, in a low voice, "us working illegally and still having no money, all of that, I feel privileged."

"Yep." Pantelis spreads his hands. "Welcome to Cyprus."

"Right," Androulla says, "where Cypriots are white and Greeks are even whiter."

He chokes laughing at this, then stubs out his cigarette and turns serious again. "Culturally, yes. We idolise the Greeks. But on a material level, I'm not sure. I see a lot of Cypriots looking down on them, now that they're finding higher salaries here."

Androulla takes a sip of her coffee. It warms her throat, just as another shower starts to spatter her ankle. She draws it in under the table.

"Do you want to move?" Pantelis asks, reaching for the sides of his chair again.

"It's okay," Androulla says, as the rain patters down upon the awning. "I'm covered. It'll probably stop again, anyway."

Pantelis releases his chair. "It's funny, you've reminded me . . . You know I studied in Norwich, right? English Literature with Creative Writing."

"Yeah," Androulla says, wrapping her hands around her coffee cup.

"So, there was another Cypriot on my course. A British-Cypriot, born and raised in London. We were debating the context of a book once, and I started my sentence with, 'As a white person . . .'"

Androulla gives half a smile.

"I couldn't understand why everyone was staring at me until after class, when the British-Cypriot . . . Kypros was his name."

"Right," Androulla says.

"Diaspora," Pantelis says, with a flare of his round eyes. "He approached me, Kypros, and said it was because of my accent that people were surprised when I called myself white."

Recalling her parents' experiences, Androulla nods.

"Then he said that as a person of Cypriot heritage, he would never consider himself white. He actually seemed offended that I did," Pantelis frowns, lifting his coffee cup.

"Oh, you embarrassed him," Androulla says. "You took away his claim to 'otherness' in front of his friends."

"Really?" Pantelis asks, lowering his cup without taking a sip. "Do you think that's why?"

"Yes," she confirms. "If he was going around proclaiming his hardships as a Cypriot, and someone demonstrably 'more Cypriot' than him came along and called themselves white . . ." She raises her eyebrows. "He would have lost some credibility there, in his mind."

"But as you were saying," Pantelis argues, extending his hand, "in Cyprus, I am white. I get treated with exceptional privilege, compared to African immigrants or even people from the north, in some places. Once I'd been in the UK longer, I understood what Kypros was saying. But it's all relative to where you are in the world."

"And when. And who with," Androulla agrees.

"Exactly," Pantelis says, drawing another cigarette from his pack.

"See, that's what I wanted to get at with my book," Androulla says. "Things like, someone who's poor in England can be privileged here. Someone who's poor here can be privileged in Sri Lanka. The relativity of that kind of stuff."

"But remember," Pantelis says, holding his cigarette unlit between two fingers, "not only are things relative between countries, they're in flux within them all the time. Every society is made up of people, growing and changing. Maybe you feel bad about how you portrayed certain things. Okay," he shrugs. "You'll do better next time. Be more informed, and write like it. You'll probably be proud of your next book, until your way of thinking shifts again and you wish you'd written it differently. That's life as an artist."

"Yeah," Androulla says, staring into the depths of her coffee.

Pantelis's lighter sparks into flame.

"You are an artist," he persists, catching her eye.

It is only as she is smiling back at him, coyly, that Androulla remembers she is wearing no makeup. And that is fine, she reminds herself. It doesn't matter that Pantelis looked disappointed the day she told him she was not just in a relationship, but married. She doesn't have to pay him back for his time or his kindness with anything but her own. He is here because she is his friend, and because she is an artist.

"Thank you," she says, as the rain ceases to fall.

The woman in lipstick, she notices, has gone.

THE FOURTEENTH

CREAKING OPEN, ANDROULLA'S WARDROBE gives out the scent of lavender moth repellent like a stale perfume. She holds her breath as she leans inside, then steps back with a dress in hand. The sound of the rain resumes in her ears, pummelling the pavements beyond her lowered blinds. She lifts her dress up to the ceiling light. Wherever else she has worn it since, she still associates this garment with Immigration. Its low neckline, its slim fit and its lustful pigment. She drags the fabric over her hips, already wearing a matching lipstick. Kostas has been unable to take this time off from his tutoring job, and so she must beg at the gates to Immigration alone.

In the harsh light of her bathroom mirror, Androulla faces herself. Overdone for the daytime, holding her arms away from her sides. She is a picture of her worst proclivities, dressed up for others' benefit. But that can't matter now, she reminds herself.

Her visa is almost out. Any self-betterment must wait until she is secure in her home country.

In her black boots and raincoat, with her tote bag full of documents, Androulla steps out. The stairwell smells of petrichor and echoes with her footsteps. Two cats are curled up against the bottom door. She makes sorry eye contact with one before following them out into the rain. It batters at her hood until she is shut inside her car, then barks at the doors. She turns the radio up loud.

An anti-immigrant rally has turned violent in Limassol. Ten minutes into their march, some two-hundred far-right demonstrators began shouting, "Cyprus is Greek". Several wore balaclavas, brandished signs saying 'Refugees not welcome' and attacked passing foreigners. Five migrant-run businesses have reported damages, the broadcaster says.

As he goes on to describe the bins and cars left burning in the protesters' wake, Androulla turns off the radio. The rain drums down upon her roof. Surrounding drivers beep and swerve. She feels her breath filling her car until she turns up the side road behind Omonoia FC and pulls her key from the engine. The car shudders into stillness.

"Okay," she says, to steady herself.

Without the windscreen wipers going, her view of a nearby pomegranate tree blurs. What would Kostas check for now?

"Passport," Androulla says, taking her bag from the passenger seat. "Photocopies of parents' passports, proof of address . . . birth certificate and adoption papers."

She lingers over these last two documents, one proclaiming her Androulla Dixon, daughter of Gary, and the other Androulla Demetriou, daughter of Kostas. Olympia has been her only constant, on paper and in practice. Androulla traces her fingertips over the name. Things would be so much easier if she could accept her mother and her Greekness, if she could settle for being a European citizen before a Cypriot one. She could stop forging proof of a shared address with her parents, marry her husband and live without fear. There is a block, something stopping her. For the sake of ease, Androulla has tried to push it aside. But she cannot shake her mother's disdain for the 'unclean' speech of the people she loves most, or dismiss her sinking feeling at the sight of Greek flags outside Cypriot houses. It is a feeling that Androulla associates with seeing the Union Jacks fly in favour of Brexit, a wretched frustration with her neighbours. Can't they see the beauty of their country? An island with the bridges of free trade and movement to Europe, but with its own identity yet. News of the Limassol protest echoes in Androulla's ears, and she vaults from her car. The far-right may never attack her physically, but its hostility towards third-country nationals alarms her. Just as England's anti-immigrant jargon injured her parents, despite them being some of 'the good ones'.

Locking her car, Androulla starts up the hill to Immigration. Her tight dress forces her to take small steps, while her boots knock into each other. With her hood up, she cannot discern the cries of workers on the apartment building still under construction. She keeps her head bowed until she is rounding the back of the Migration Department, then unzips her coat.

"*Chaírete*," she calls, to a security officer beyond the bars.

His dark eyes slide over her as she approaches. Ignoring the stares of applicants huddling beneath the metal shelter to her left, Androulla gives him a smile.

"*Kaliméra*," he says, without returning it.

She clears her throat. "I'm in the process of applying to renew my 'extended stay' here?"

The officer looks at her, blankly.

"I had an appointment on twenty-seventh of November, and they told me to come back with my documents . . ."

"Do you have an appointment today?" he asks.

She tightens her grip on her bag strap. "No. They didn't tell me I'd need one."

"You always need an appointment," the officer says, taking a backwards step, "whatever you're doing."

"I don't need to see anyone," Androulla persists, stepping after him.

The metallic smell of the bars fills her nostrils like blood.

"It won't take up any time. I'm just here to drop off . . ."

"I can't let you in," the officer maintains, shaking his head.

The sound of the rain hitting the shelter rings through Androulla's ears.

"Well, can I leave them with you?" she asks.

"Hey," a second officer calls, motioning towards the gate.

Androulla watches it swing open for another eastern European-looking girl, then clank shut again. Heart thumping, she peels her bag off her shoulder and her raincoat with it, exposing her skin to the cool air.

"Let me show you," she says, as the dark-eyed officer looks back at her.

She leans to inspect her bag's contents, giving him full view of her cleavage. As she inhales, her breasts swell between her tight dress and her push-up bra. Her ring finger is bare again, after all the progress she has made. She hates herself.

"It's these," she says, unclenching her jaw as she lifts out a plastic wallet.

Without glancing at it, the officer shakes his head again. Androulla feels her hood trembling under the rain.

"I'm not able to take any paperwork. You'll need to go home and book an appointment," the officer repeats.

He turns away, leaving her chest to gape open.

"But," she starts.

This is the dress she wore last summer, that saw her inside without an appointment. Her visa expiry date is looming as large now as it was then, but she cannot see the officer who understood that, or at the very least indulged it. Dropping back onto her heels, Androulla stows away her documents. She tucks her shoulder into her coat sleeve and feels like she is sweating. Like her mascara is running, stinging her eyes. She wipes them. Turning away from the bars, she meets the quiet, knowing stares of the people beneath the shelter. She wants to curse them for witnessing her assumption of privilege, her regression to 'object'. To clutch their hands and weep for the awfulness of it all.

But she doubts they would allow her to without sneering, because the security officer didn't ignore her when she called out. He didn't take one look and turn away, because Androulla is white. Everyone who is supposed to love her seems to love reminding her of this fact more. Her stepfather, particularly, since he was called 'Paki' by youths on the Jubilee Line and told to 'go back now' by newly victorious Brexiteers. No, with her clear English voice and her European hair, Androulla has never been made to feel like she is of an 'inferior race', that is true. But in Cyprus it matters very much where you are from, in every case. There is a distrust of foreigners – particularly those with pale skin, Androulla feels – due to its long history of being colonised. Leftover is a kind of reproachful admiration for the Greek and the English. Despite its independence, Cyprus maintains its reverence for 'clean' Greek and the prestigious English School. Androulla doesn't want to be associated with either.

She wants to say, "I'm Cypriot. By dissension, like you. Not by the happenstance of my mother's love, or by virtue of hanging around to get my status by time-spent. I am Cypriot. As true a member of my family as you are of yours."

She stumbles around the corner, fumbling to do up her coat. When the zip catches, she stops. Undoes it. Blinks her vision clear and tries again. Again, the zip gets stuck a third of the way up her body. Androulla falters. It could be that today's officer was not one swayed by sexual provocation. Or, she realises, it could be that he was not swayed by her. That for all her determination to eat right and get well, in recent weeks, she has filled out her dress in a way that no longer appeals. Androulla unfurls, ripping open her coat. She has let Giannis convince her several times that any weight again she sees is in her head. But Giannis loves her. What if he is just trying to be nice?

With dripping hair, Androulla climbs into their car. It takes three attempts to start, doing so with a splutter. At a red light, she sniffs. She won't eat lunch today. Or tomorrow, or the next day, or the day after that.

THE TWENTY-FIFTH

ANDROULLA DETESTS CHRISTMAS DAY from its break. The rain strikes her as fitting, coming down in fine points beyond her window.

"Merry Christmas, Wife," Giannis's voice sounds, muffled by bed sheets.

Releasing the blind, Androulla turns and softens at the sight of him, nestled up to her pillow.

"You always move onto my side," she says, once she has returned his Christmas wishes.

"It smells like you," he says, hugging her pillow closer.

She sinks onto the edge of the mattress. "What do I smell like?"

Giannis opens his eyes. "Just skin and, I don't know. Familiar." He rolls away, stretching his arms up over his head. Through a yawn, he asks, "Is this how it feels to get a full night's sleep? My god."

Stifling a yawn of her own, Androulla lays a hand on his chest. "I'm glad we had last night together. I wish you didn't have to work today, though."

"I don't, until five," Giannis says. "And you'll be with your family."

"Exactly," Androulla reminds him, with arched eyebrows.

"You love your cousins," he persists.

She sighs. "I do, until it's an end-of-year, taking-stock kind of event. And then we all get compared on who's dating, who's engaged, who's married . . ."

"You win, then," Giannis grins.

"Well, yeah. This year," Androulla says. "But if we have to compete, shouldn't it be for, like, who's got the best job or who can afford the biggest house?"

"In theory, of course it should," Giannis says. "But I'm afraid you'd lose in all those categories. As would I," he laughs, as she brings her palm down upon his chest.

They wrestle each other with tickling fingers until Giannis's phone rings.

"It's my mum," he warns.

Seeing that it is a video call, Androulla dives off the bed.

"Merry Christmas, *to ómorfo agóri mou*," sounds a nasal voice.

"How are you going, *Mamá*?" her 'beautiful boy' asks, glaring at Androulla over the top of his phone.

She motions to her bare face, her unbrushed hair and her braless chest, then slips from the room.

"We've just put on the *foukoú*, the barbie, for dinner," her mother-in-law starts.

Androulla drowns out her voice by filling the kettle. The terrazzo floor is cold beneath her feet, the window speckled with rain to match. It is important to all Giannis's family that he is fighting for his right to their ancestral homeland, of course. Yet how dare Androulla drag him away to suffer so many hardships? Closing the lid, she sets the kettle to boil. Her mother-in-law would rather that Giannis was close-by than happy, she knows. This is not an uncommon trait in Mediterranean mothers. Androulla will send a nice message later, when she has had the warm-up of wishing her own relatives well. The kettle quietens to a simmer and she pours it into two instant coffees.

"You're lucky to have your family here," Giannis says, when they sit down to breakfast.

"I know," Androulla acknowledges.

She shuffles a worn deck of playing cards while he crunches into his toast. She is saving herself for lunch, she assures him.

They get to her grandparents' after noon, bearing a bottle of red wine that Androulla still thinks was too expensive. The olive leaf wreath folds away from them.

"Come in," her grandmother says, squinting out at the rain. "Not exactly a white Christmas, but there is something falling," she chuckles, when they are safe inside.

The house smells as Cyprus does every Sunday, with the smoke rising from its domed ovens, of lamb languishing in garlic, oregano, rosemary, lemon juice and olive oil. Bouzouki music flourishes from the kitchen. Androulla's grandmother ushers them towards it, just as a male vocalist begins warbling and laughter erupts. Unsure of the joke, Androulla stops in the kitchen doorway.

"*Kalá Christoúgenna,*" Giannis calls out, supporting the small of her back.

With bright smiles, Androulla's relatives turn to greet them. She kisses them each in turn, first her Uncle Stavros, her step-father's brother, and his wife Georgia. Then their daughters, Christina and Niki, who are respectively twenty-nine and en-gaged, and twenty-four with a long-term boyfriend, though neither man is present today. Androulla's grandfather ap-proaches her next, and looks horrified when she tells him yet again that she will drink just water.

"Are you sure you're not pregnant?" he asks, prodding her stomach.

Her laughter comes out breathless.

Next to arrive are Androulla's parents, her mother bearing a covered dish. There is more hugging, more kissing, more stand-ing in the kitchen with drinks, until the final arm of the family arrives. Kostas's sister Chrystalla, with her son Charis and her daughter Sofia.

"You're so thin," Sofia moans, releasing Androulla from a hug to pat down her sides. Thirty-one, thick-thighed and per-petually single, Sofia is the loser of the cousins' contest, never mind her senior position in finance. "Have you been doing the Nativity Fast?" she asks.

Their grandmother chuckles, patting Androulla on the back. "Don't worry. She'll put some kilos today, I'm sure."

"Thank you," Androulla says, accepting her glass of water. It cools her palm.

Once everyone else has a glass of red wine or whiskey in hand, the process of ferrying dishes to the table can commence. There is egg-lemon soup, hot off the stove. One bowl piled high with hunks of chicken *soúvla*, and another with pork. Having roasted with the lamb, the potatoes come out ripe with juices. When Androulla goes back for the salad, her aunts and grandmother are cooing over something in tinfoil.

Upon noticing her, Georgia folds it back to reveal a round loaf with a cross baked into it. "Christina made a *Gennopitta*."

"A *Christopsomo*," Olympia corrects her, quietly.

"Wow," Androulla musters, as the sweet, nutty fragrance of the bread fills her nostrils. Remembering the dish that her mother arrived with, she stands back. "Should I have made something too? I feel bad."

"You are our guest, Androulla *mou*," her grandmother says, sending her back to the table with a pat on the back. "Leave the preparations to the older generations."

As their laughter follows her into the dining room, Androulla struggles to understand what qualifies Christina as the 'older' cousin, when she is two years Sofia's junior and only three Androulla's senior. Anguish twists through her veins at the label 'guest', which the government is doing its utmost to hold her to. She shuffles her chair close to Giannis's.

When they are all seated, her grandfather raises his whiskey. "Cheers, everyone. Thank you for coming. *Kalá Christoúgenna!*"

"Merry Christmas!" the family echoes, over the clinking of glasses and the trilling of *bouzoúkia*.

Androulla feels Kostas watching her as they pass the dishes around. She takes a generous helping of salad, spreading it over half her plate, and then realises that no one has thought to bring bowls for the egg-lemon soup. As her grandmother refutes her offer to fetch some, her stepfather drops a potato onto her salad, flattening the parsley.

"What? You don't want one?" he responds, to her glare.

For some moments, no one speaks except to proffer, request or praise the offerings upon the table. The *kléftiko* is a big success.

"Did you take some, Androulla?" Chrystalla asks.

"I'll get there," Androulla says, through a mimed mouthful. "One course at a time."

Her relatives laugh.

"So, Christina. How is the wedding planning going? Have you decided on a date yet?" Olympia asks.

As the only mother without a stake in the marriage race, she appears genuinely interested in the answer. Chrystalla's lips look thin as she slows her chewing, while Georgia's turn up with pride.

"It won't be for a while yet," Christina says, lowering her fork. "We want to take a few months to . . . see the lay of the land, I think." Catching her mother's eye, she smiles and looks down at her plate.

A weight drops to the pit of Androulla's stomach. Perhaps if it weren't for her infertility, she wouldn't have caught the implication. Perhaps she is oversensitive and imagining it altogether, she thinks, as she scrapes the filling of her potato out of its jacket and around her plate.

"Show me the ring again, Christina *mou*," her grandmother says, leaning over. "It's so beautiful. He has good taste . . ."

When the table is a graveyard of scattered remains, the women get up to clear it. Androulla isn't conscious of the imbalance until she is standing in the kitchen with a stack of plates, waiting for her grandmother to assign her next task. Around her are her aunts, her mother, and all her cousins except for Charis. The only man to enter the room is Giannis, with two empty wine glasses, and Chrystalla chases him out. Androulla's grandmother hands her a tea towel, thin with wear.

"We do this," Sofia mutters, pulling a plate from the washing up bowl, "while they sit around and play cards. Every year," she adds, for emphasis.

"I know," Androulla says.

Despite the injustice of it, she cannot commit, wholeheartedly, to an eye roll like her cousin's. Androulla grew up displaced, sticking to old Cypriot ways even when she didn't agree with them. In any case, if she did speak out it wouldn't be about the sexism. That is straightforward, anyone could do it and surely, before long, they will. Androulla dries the plate and hands it off to Niki. What she wants to say is that she doesn't understand what defines a woman. Could someone tell her, please? Because if it is a tolerance for housework, a lack of testosterone or the capacity for motherhood, then she is in the wrong room. She takes a fistful of dripping forks from Sofia, and pricks herself on one of their prongs.

"You're bleeding," Niki says, cupping her thumb. "Go and wash your hands, I'll do this."

"Sorry. Thank you," Androulla mumbles.

Leaving her aunts to fuss in her wake, she makes for the bathroom. On her way there, she hears the distinctive table-slamming of her male relatives playing *Pilotta*. They are sitting at a square table, her grandfather and Stavros on one team, and Kostas and Charis on the other. The father without a son and the son without a father, Androulla thinks, as she glimpses Kostas whispering and pointing at Charis's cards. Giannis is standing over them, brow furrowed as he watches as though he, too, feels out of place. Androulla locks her urge to run away with him behind the bathroom door.

With her palms braced upon the sink, she lets out a breath. The music sounds fainter in here, the laughter somehow clearer. Hearing Christina's, Androulla recalls the extra care that pregnant women must take over the Twelve Days of Christmas, according to legends of the *kalikantzaroi*. Any child born during the time when those malevolent creatures crawl up from the underworld, annually, must be bound in tresses of garlic or straw, or have their toenails singed, to stop them from turning.

Androulla will never have to worry about that. She runs cold water over her thumb, rubbing it hard. The horrors of the *kalikantzaroi* will not touch her adult life, any more than the joys of Father Christmas will.

Her thumb feels raw when she ceases her scrubbing. Rinsing her blood down the drain, Androulla stumbles out of the bathroom and into her husband.

"You scared me," she breathes.

Giannis's eyes follow her hand to her heart. "Georgia said you'd cut yourself."

"Oh, yeah. Not badly," Androulla says, looking down at her thumb.

A raw patch of skin shadows the inside of her nail. Giannis kisses it.

"I have to go," he says.

"Do you?" she asks, keeping hold of his hand.

"Sorry." He pulls her in for a hug. "Kostas says he'll drop you home later."

"Okay," Androulla says, as they draw apart. "I'll walk you out."

As she is waving him off in their car, her phone chimes. Pulling it from her pocket, she smiles at a 'season's greetings' text from Naomi, then sees that she has a voicemail. The rain is still falling, steadily, forcing her to stand close to the wall of her grandparents' house. A drop lands upon her nose as she lifts her phone, and hears that she has a new message.

"Hi Andy, it's Dad," Gary's voice sounds, after the beep. "I'm not sure what time it is where you are. We're sitting down for lunch here. Anyway, just wanted to say happy Christmas. Give your old man a call back, if you like."

THE TWENTY-EIGHTH

AFTER SUBMITTING HER FIRST draft of another undergraduate essay, Androulla minimises her tab. Beyond her living room window, it is raining needles. She opens files, selects 'Copper' and stares at the opening line of her novel. Then she returns to work.

The Twenty-Ninth

WITH GIANNIS OUT, THE day's washing up consists of a single coffee cup. Beyond the kitchen window, the Pentadaktylos Mountains are shrouded in fog. Androulla slides it open to hear the pattering rain and feel the wind upon her face. Leaving her cup upside-down on the draining board, she starts to make dinner. Beans again.

THE THIRTY-FIRST

CHRISTMAS IS OVER. THAT is what the rain says, coming down like rice after a wedding ceremony. Remembering hers, Androulla feels both affirmed and false. Christmas is over, along with the most turbulent year of her life.

Letting the blind fall back over their bedroom window, she watches her husband's chest rise and fall. Tonight Giannis will get double pay for working at the bar, while Androulla sees in the New Year with her parents' friends. She doesn't want to, particularly, but she was infected years ago with a superstition of her stepmother's. If she didn't do something to welcome the year, then how was it going to welcome her? She thinks of New Year's Eves that she spent with Naomi, before Oscar passed away. Of Christmases divided between her mother's and her father's. New Year's Days when her resolution was to stop eating, and New Year's Days when it was to start again.

One December, she and her parents went to Belgium for a long weekend. Kostas had some holiday left, and it was clear they would have to do something different that year. Androulla had outgrown their old traditions and Olympia was taking this hard, intermittently snapping and sulking. They couldn't be in a room together without falling out, nor could they afford to spend Christmas with their relatives in Cyprus or Rhodes. And so Bruges it was.

They got a deal on a family room, with one double bed and one narrower than single, pushed up underneath a window. The pane was thin and faced out onto a dank alleyway, a short walk from Market Square.

"Wrap up warm," Olympia said. "Gloves, hat, scarf . . ."

Androulla was newly starving herself and furious that no one had noticed yet. She looked ridiculous with her overlarge mittens, bobble hat and chunky scarf layered over her skinny jeans. Like one of those bobble-head figures that sat grinning upon a dashboard.

She reminded herself of how important it was to preserve this look as they emerged into the cobbled square, where the scents of buttery waffles and hot chocolates rose from wooden stalls. The surrounding buildings looked like facades that had been propped up for the festivities, with red and purple bricks climbing up stairs to triangular roofs, and arched windows framing fir trees.

Against the biting cold, Androulla bowed into her scarf. She had been unable to touch herself the previous night, in the room with her parents, and she knew it was affecting her mood. As was her mother's presence, generally. As was the watering of her mouth as they passed by stalls selling choco-late-covered walnuts and amaretto truffles.

"Do you want to try one, Androulla *mou*?" Olympia asked, holding up the traffic as she stopped to point.

"No," Androulla snapped, more at herself than at her mother.

Someone ploughed into the back of her and she apol-ogised, sheepishly, then glared at Olympia. Kostas was mouthing something from the next stall, standing up on his toes to wave them over. As they shuffled towards him, Androulla saw a wooden sign slotted in among tubes of sausage meat, which read, 'En = Duck'. She was caught be-tween two speakers, Wham! in conflict with Michael Bublé, drowning out her parents' debate. Androulla gathered that it had something to do with the cost of the duck meat.

With a jingle, her mother swept her into one of the shops that bordered the square. The smell of roasting chestnuts gave way to one of plastic packaging, the music to a version of 'Jingle Bells' sung by a children's choir. Androulla ran her eyes over shelves of steel water bottles and pegs of canvas bags. A generalised gift shop, she surmised. The space felt wide open after the crowded market, with only Olympia sifting through a basket of pencil cases.

Androulla pawed at her elbow. "*Mamá*," she said, quietly.

"Mmn," her mother mused, weighing a pouch patterned with unicorns in her palm. "Do you think Niki would like this?" she asked.

"Yeah, maybe. But *Mamá*," Androulla repeated, with growing urgency. "I have a weird pain . . ."

Olympia half-turned towards her. "You have a weird pain," she murmured, her voice curving up to a peak just shy of curious.

"It's in my side, here," Androulla persisted.

She indicated the right-hand side of her lower abdomen where something was writhing – grasping at her insides for help, she felt – as it withered and died.

"It's like a stitch, but . . ."

She couldn't bring herself to say that it was hurting her in the same way her period might, only at a pitch high enough to make her grit her teeth. She was fourteen. The thought of anyone knowing about her period, even the friends who told her about theirs with scrunched eyes and cradled stomachs, mortified Androulla. But she wasn't on it now, nor was she due to be anytime soon. This wasn't right.

"*Mamá*," she said again, doubling over as a flare of pain shot sparks through the dark sky of her torso.

"Yes, *agápi mou*. Just let me pay for this and then we can find somewhere to sit, okay?" Again, Olympia's voice came up just short of a real question.

While she made brittle small talk with the man behind the counter, Androulla stumbled outside. The jingle of the doorbell rattled around inside her ear with her mother's voice, calling after her. There were cold-pinched faces and catching shoulders. Then Androulla was on a low wall or the step up to another shop, she wasn't sure. She could see nothing above the thick socks and boots of people marching by, hear nothing above the sound of her own ragged breaths.

"Androulla," her mother's voice broke through, sharper now. "Where are you?" she barked, into her phone.

Kostas was with them moments later, crouching down by Androulla's side. "*Moró mou*," he said, touching her back, "my baby. What's wrong? Did something happen?"

With the moisture gone from her mouth, Androulla could do nothing but shake her head.

"She said she had a pain. Where was it, Androulla? Can you show us?" her mother asked.

By now, the flare had set alight the great forest of her insides. It was ripping through from her shoulders to her thighs, making her throat close up. She made a circular motion across her upper body, then returned to bracing her hands against the hard ground. Even as she bit down, a cry escaped her and people looked, Androulla sensed them. It didn't matter. Her parents hauled her up and away from the square to search for a pharmacy. She whimpered with every step and they said they knew, they were sorry but they were going to get her to help. Their voices were too full of alarm to be soothing.

"Closed," Kostas declared the first pharmacy, when its door would not budge. And the second.

"They're all on Christmas hours," Olympia fretted.

Androulla sank halfway to her knees before her stepfather caught her.

"You can't collapse here. Go back to the room with *Mamá*," he urged her, "and I'll keep looking."

Thirty minutes later, he shouldered through the door of their family room to break the news of his discovery. In Belgium, painkillers could not be bought over the counter, not even the weakest varieties. Androulla would have to ride out whatever this was until they were back in England. Olympia started on Kostas as if he had made this rule, only stopping when Androulla begged her with a wordless groan. The springs of her mattress were digging into her side, the duvet stifling her even as she shivered.

For a night and a day, she did not move from her curled up state. She drifted in and out of a fitful sleep while her parents took turns to watch her and browse the market stalls. At one point, the trumpeting of a marching band woke her and she covered her head. Then it was their final morning and silent, as if a snow had fallen. It hadn't. Nothing about the trip had gone to festive accord, and the six-hour drive home was bitter. Dropping Olympia off with their bags, Kostas took Androulla to hospital.

Two weeks later, a doctor called them back to review Androulla's ultrasound. In an office choking with antibacterial fumes, he explained that a cyst on her ovary had ruptured.

"Can you see that shadow, there?" he said, pointing. "That's where the cyst was still breaking down. The pain you experienced would have been caused by the toxic fluid from inside it getting into your bloodstream."

Androulla leaned away from the sonogram. It sounded awful, like something that she would never recover from. But it wasn't, the doctor assured her. She would be fine. He didn't tell her it would not be a one-off ordeal, that her ovaries were in fact *poly*cystic and would erupt into agony time and again. Within ten years, they would be as barren as the land after a forest fire, for their scarring. They would show up on scans looking porous, like natural sponges. Three other doctors would see them and diagnose the problem, but even they wouldn't explain it beyond listing the most common symptoms. Bad skin. Irregular periods. Hairy forearms. Oh, and infertility, especially with damage as bad as Androulla's. Have a nice day.

Her husband rolls onto his side, his eyes flickering open. "Is it snowing?" he asks.

Androulla looks at the beaded cord, still swinging beside the blind. Blinking, she moves it aside again, letting in a slice of white light. The rain is still scattering down as though from the palm of a hand. The leaves of orange and lemon trees are turning a vibrant green, thriving now that summer is over. Unlike in England, it is the heat and not the cold that drives most trees here to drop their leaves. This makes sense, though Androulla is still getting used to it. This inversion of the natural order as she grew up understanding it.

"It's raining," she says, as she releases the blind.

"Oh. I heard it was going to snow last night," Giannis murmurs, into her pillow.

Vaguely, Androulla nods. "Maybe in Troodos," she says.

JANUARY

The Fifth

BETWEEN ASSIGNMENTS, ANDROULLA SHUTS down her laptop. She has worked all morning with a palm braced against her
abdomen, hearing the rain lash at the window and gritting her
teeth. The pain shifts with her as she stands up, doubling its
span. She grips the table, catching her breath. Then makes for
the door.

She bundles into her winter coat. Like a double quilt on a
single bed, it overhangs her knees, thick black. She almost did
away with it when she moved to Cyprus, not understanding,
since her prior visits had been in summertime, how cold it could
be in the winter months. She used to wear it to her job of
blue-skying house photos and bow her chin into its collar. But
she took it off when she got inside, to the central heating of her
parents' home or of the greasy-smelling office. It is painstaking
to shed this layer in Cyprus, amid so many high ceilings and tiled
floors. Radiators are a rarity, with the nation geared towards

summertime. Instead, Androulla sets her air conditioner to exhaling heat until her face feels dry, the room smells stuffy and she cannot breathe. Then she turns it off and huddles with Giannis around a whining electric heater, which affects nothing but the immediate space. Sex has become difficult to orchestrate, with both of them gasping when the duvet lifts.

With her arms shrieking past her sides, Androulla sets out in the rain. The further down she tilts her chin, the more water slides past her face. Within moments, her hands feel raw and she tucks them into her pockets, opening and closing her fists to get their feeling back. Still, the ache in her abdomen spurs her on. Giannis wasn't home to make this trip for her and she hated the thought of waiting, for his shift to end or for the weather to let up, with their cheap toilet paper disintegrating in her underwear. She looks up to cross the road and a raindrop hits her eye, making her blink. Because her period is unpredictable, she is seldom prepared for it. Perhaps that should have been her New Year's resolution, she thinks. To keep a war chest of tampons and never again be caught short, with the warning of cramps mere hours before she bled.

"*Geiá sas*," the portly man greets her, inside the pharmacy.

Androulla gives him a weak smile and turns towards the shelves. Feeling his eyes follow her, she makes a show of cradling her ovarian region. She hears a murmur as she stops to collect herself, reading the labels of irrelevant products. Sun sprays, sun creams and sunscreens, lined up in brightly coloured bottles. She takes a deep breath of ethanol and something like lemon balm. Footsteps sound and then the curly-haired girl is upon her, in another swampy-looking jumper.

"*Chaírete*. Would you like some help?" she asks, in her loud voice.

"No. Thank you, I'm fine," Androulla smiles, encouragingly.

When the girl doesn't move, she insists with a nod.

"If you change your mind, you can tell me. Okay?" the girl says, as she backs away.

"*Efcharistó*, thank you . . ."

Still nodding, Androulla turns her back to the counter. Hot air blows at her from a unit overhead and she moves along, lips pursed. She still can't see what Giannis found attractive about this girl, with her lack of spatial awareness or volume control, and her terrible dress sense. Sometimes his taste makes Androulla question herself, more even than usual. Recalling his suspicion that the curly-haired girl liked him, too, Androulla feels worlds away from the person she was last summer. Like she is seeing her husband's old fancy through a pane of glass, where once she stood out and tasted the breeze of it.

Picking up as many sanitary towels as she can for as little money, Androulla steps up to the counter. It appears that the tall girl, who she liked, no longer works here.

"*Efcharistó*," the stern-eyed man thanks her. "Have a nice day."

"And you," Androulla says, pulling her hood back over her head.

She slots her supplies into the bathroom when she gets home, and the cramps persist. But her period does not come.

THE TWELFTH

ANDROULLA STARES AT THE test, still in its box. A thin cardboard rectangle depicting something that she thought looked like a thermometer, the first time she saw one. She was in Boots with her mother, a week after her night with Oscar, and terrified that she could test positive. That the sight of his naked body could have rooted itself inside hers, to grow outwards and give her away. The longer her mother browsed the products beside the tests, the hotter Androulla's cheeks turned.

"Okay. Ready?" Olympia asked, standing back.

Androulla hadn't noticed her take anything from the shelf. She blinked and nodded, profusely. Her mother gave a small frown before she went to pay, without looking twice.

Rain patters down beyond the slanted bathroom window. Unboxing the test, Androulla sighs. She feels none of the fluttering, nervous excitement that she imagines she would if she were dreading a pregnancy, or hoping for one. Her hands are steady. She is sure, as she takes the instructions like a cigarette between two fingers, that this is unnecessary. Cruel, even. A waste of her time. She struggles to read in the dreary afternoon light, and yellows the room with its bare bulb. The ache persists in her lower abdomen, as it has for days. She might have laughed at herself, hollowly, as she bought this test. But it is somewhere to start, ruling out explanations for her bloodless pain.

When she has read over the instructions a second time, Androulla folds them away. She slides out the test and cringes at the squealing rip of its plastic wrapper, then uncaps one end of it. A thin white tab protrudes. Quashing her urge to hold it under her tongue, she squats over the toilet.

She thinks she waits five seconds before jerking the test out from under her. Fumbling for the cap, she balances it on the edge of the sink and sets a three-minute timer. When it trills, Androulla is watching the rain, coming down just thicker than mist. She turns to silence her phone.

Her next inhalation webs her lungs. The sound of the rain fills her ears and she slams the window shut, then picks up the test. Her hand is trembling, making the result hard to read. She steadies herself. Another look at the instructions confirms it. There, in the left-half of the rectangular screen, is the control line. And to its right, the slightest discoloration.

A knock on the door sends her hand to her chest.

"How are you going in there?" Giannis calls.

Androulla jolts to recover the test. "Fine. I just, erm . . ." she starts.

The door handle slips her grasp as she stumbles backwards, facing her husband. He blinks at her, fresh-smelling for his PhD meeting.

"Is that a line?" She holds up the test.

Bending to read it, he frowns.

"Yes or no?" she frets.

He tuts, snatching it. "I can't see when you're shaking it around."

Biting her thumbnail, Androulla watches him lift it up to the bathroom light, then take it out into the hallway. Slowly, he turns back.

"What do you think?" she asks.

"I don't know. If that is a line, I can barely see it," he says, looking up.

Androulla takes the test back from him. "Maybe it's, like, the outline of where the line is supposed to show. If you are pregnant," she says.

Giannis is still staring at the thing, clutched between her fingers. Something inside her sinks at the twist of his lips, her hope or her fear, whatever it is that she is feeling.

"I don't know if it works like that," he admits. He runs his hands through his hair. "I don't know, I don't . . ."

Androulla turns to collect the plastic wrapper and other packaging.

"What are you doing?" Giannis asks, lowering his arms.

"Throwing this stuff away."

"Wait, don't do that–"

The corner bin clanks open, its steel lid against the tiled wall. Androulla drops the test in and lets it fall shut again.

"The results aren't valid for more than a few minutes," she says, slipping past her husband.

He steps after her into the hallway. "Where are you going?"

"To buy more tests."

"Do you want me to come with you?"

Androulla looks up from lacing her boots. Giannis is standing a pace away, a wary look upon his face. The adolescent in him wants to flee from her tell-tale body, she realises, just as she wants to silence it. As teenagers, they both learned to fear implication in any pregnancies. Then they got married, and it was all their aunts and uncles could do not to chase them to bed. Androulla blushed, then blanched when she discovered her infertility. And now this. It has all been so sudden, so sweeping, so shocking that she can no longer place her feelings on pregnancy. Is it sinful? A blessing reserved for other, better women? Or is it about to reveal itself, equal parts miracle and disaster? She eyes its bringer, cagily.

"Don't you have to leave?" she asks.

"I'm hardly going to do that now, am I?" Giannis responds, as if slighted.

Extending a hand, he pulls her upright.

"Thank you," she mumbles.

They walk in silence to the pharmacy, Androulla for the third time since she thought she would bleed and proceeded not to. Despite her stable relationship and her relative safety from the 'young mum' tag, she fears judgement from the pharmacist and his curly-haired assistant.

"Will you go in?" she asks her husband, when they reach the green storefront.

"Okay, yeah." He falls back a step, squinting upwards. "I'm not sure what I'm looking for. Is there a certain brand, or .. ?"

"Any, it doesn't matter. Just find a cheap one and get a few. Thank you," she calls, as the doors slide shut behind him.

The rain falls like a veil before Androulla's eyes. She touches the lymph node still swollen in her neck. She can barely see across the road by the time Giannis reappears, plastic bag in hand.

She asks him to wait outside the bathroom while she takes a second test. And a third. Neither one presents them with a clearer answer.

"What are you doing?" Giannis asks, as Androulla angles her phone.

She snaps a picture. "Getting a second opinion."

Naomi responds to her message in under a minute, with a phone call and the words, "Oh my god."

"Hi," Androulla greets her, leaning her back against the shower panel.

"Well, I wasn't expecting that . . ."

"Neither was I . . ."

Giannis rolls his eyes, motioning for her to speed up the introductions.

"So, what do you think?" she asks her sister. "You're on loudspeaker, by the way. Giannis is here."

"Oh, hey," Naomi greets him.

"How are you going," he says, impatiently.

Naomi gives a sigh that resounds through their bathroom. "I don't know what to make of it, really. There should be another line next to that dark one, right? If it's positive."

"Yeah, on the right-hand side," Androulla says. She zooms in on the image. "Can you see that very faint . . ? It's barely a shadow . . ."

"I can see something, but. I don't know if I'd call it a line," Naomi says, carefully.

"No." Looking from the picture to the test, upturned on the sink, Androulla bites her lip.

"Can I ask, do you want it to be a line?" her sister asks. "I mean, are you hoping . . ?"

There is a shift in the room, the muffled clearing of a throat. Androulla looks sideways at Giannis. His head is bowed, his hair wet from their walk to the pharmacy. Pushing it back, he returns her gaze. If there is hope in his eyes, it is as faint as the line.

"We just want an answer, I think," she says, "at this stage."

He nods.

"I think it's supposed to be more accurate if you test in the morning," Naomi says.

"Actually, yeah. I've heard that," Androulla recalls, reaching for her phone. She grimaces at the time it displays.

"I know you'll be anxious waiting, but I think you should go back to the shop. And then, do they have the tests that tell you how many weeks?"

"Should do," she says.

"Okay, so get one of those and take it first thing tomorrow," Naomi advises her.

Androulla lets out a sigh.

"I know, but you'll just stress yourself out tonight if you keep–"

"You're right," she concedes. "I'll go back to the pharmacy. Thank you."

"Call me," her sister says. "And you, Gianni. If you need anything."

"Appreciate that," he says, leaning closer. "Take care."

He stands upright as Androulla ends the call. She stares up at him, lowering her phone. Between them, empty boxes and plastic packets litter the floor.

"I don't know what to say."

"Me neither," Giannis murmurs.

She drops his gaze.

"I'll go and get that test. You lie down, read your book, and then I'll make us some dinner," he says.

Androulla is halfway to protesting that she is not infirm, is not even confirmed pregnant, when she hears herself thanking him. Then remembers, "Your meeting . . ."

"Not important," he declares, taking her shoulders into his hands. "We're in this together. Okay? I'm with you."

She nods, wordlessly. He kisses her forehead and leaves their apartment.

Wrenching the bathroom window open, Androulla lets the sound of the rain grow louder again. To 'catch' a baby would be a miracle, with the frayed nets of her ovaries. One that she hasn't prepared for and cannot afford. She sinks back onto her heels. It was hard to accept that she might never get a chance at motherhood, even when she thought she didn't want one. It will be excruciating, she realises, if a single, frail opportunity presents itself, and she has to forgo it.

THE THIRTEENTH

PREGNANT. TWO-TO-THREE WEEKS, THE test says.

Androulla presses her hands to her mouth. Even as she stifles the sobs, they rock her body. She hopes the sound of the rain is loud enough outside the bathroom that Giannis can't hear the air, escaping her nose in sharp bursts. She closes her eyes. She wants to be alone. To preserve her husband's not knowing, for a moment longer.

"I'm pregnant," is not something that she ever pictured saying in tears.

With giddy laughter, perhaps, as seen on TV. Otherwise with dismay, alleviated by a pill or at worst, upon a table. But not this deep, rending feeling. It is like descending as she stands still, fast enough to break into pieces. She is pregnant. This should be said after, "Darling," "Good news," or, "I've got something to tell you."

Androulla faces the mirror. "I'm pregnant," she whispers.

The words catch in her throat. Her hair is dishevelled, and no joy reaches her eyes. How can it? Whether she wants to or not, she cannot keep this baby. Giannis will know that by looking at her. She will destroy the news of her condition in the breath she delivers it, and so she waits, holding onto it with the sides of the sink.

"Androulla?" he calls, when the end of three-minutes has rung out long enough. He knocks, gently, at the door.

"One minute."

She flushes the toilet, buying herself time to take a picture of the test. Of 'Pregnant 2-3', in the grimy join where the wall meets the sink. She doesn't know why. With her phone face-down, she lets him in.

There is a rush from the rooms that haven't aired out, from their dinner of baked eggs and beans and the air conditioner casting its stuffiness overnight. Her husband looks so vulner-able, gazing down at her out of the know, that Androulla feels monstrous. Like cradling his head and driving her own again and again into the tiled wall. She bursts into tears and Giannis takes hold of her. As she convulses against his chest, he reaches over her shoulder. She feels him straining, then hears the clatter of plastic back to porcelain. He holds her tighter. The sound of the rain envelops them.

With her nose outrunning her sniffles, Androulla pulls back. "Sorry," she says, half-covering her face.

Giannis tears off a wad of toilet roll.

"Thanks," she says, as she cleans herself up.

The bathroom bin clanks open and shut with a hollow sound.

"What are you thinking?" he murmurs.

Her gaze goes to the test, lying quiet and still.

"We can't keep it." The words break from her.

Swiping at her cheeks, she reminds him of the issues they discussed last night, with their eyes opened up to the invisible ceiling until the woodpigeons called. They are too young. They can barely sustain themselves after the rent, the bills and the unconscionable costs of immigrating. Of flying Giannis to and from Melbourne, paying to attain and apostle the many documents that were required for his student visa, and then paying for so much of his course upfront. For a second chest x-ray and round of blood tests when he returned to Cyprus and, apparently, the examinations that had been vital to his entry were nullified. For the medical insurance that would cover his health because the state would not. Any money that he or Androulla had managed to put aside was gone, by September. Back to school. A new year, a more weathered and weary Giannis, with his largest debts still looming. Nonetheless, he was a student. He would be a student for another three years. They agreed, they couldn't have a child starting school with one of them still signed up to classes. Nor could Androulla see taking on a 'dependant' when she was, legally, still classed as one herself.

Giannis drops her gaze, his throat flexing in and out. "I guess that's it, then. Decision made."

"Yeah," she says, in a hoarse voice.

Without looking up, he touches her shoulder. "Do you know what you need to do?"

"Erm. In England I'd know. Here, I'm not sure. I'll have to look into it," she says.

Nodding, he lowers his hand. Its lack is a cold shock to Androulla's shoulder.

"Gianni," she says.

He looks at her.

"What if this is our only one?"

Her voice is small, then swallowed up into his sweatshirt.

"Three doctors said this wouldn't happen." She fights her hair back, sticking with tears. "And the rate at which we've tested that theory, just to prove them wrong once . . . If we wait to be ready, we could be waiting forever. I know we've talked about adoption, but . . ."

"I'm still open to that. But it is hard to qualify, financially," Giannis admits. "And from what I've read, most agencies ask that you 'intend to remain' in your home country. And that you've been living there for at least a year, before you apply."

Androulla falls away from him. "See, in our position we just can't commit to that," she sobs.

"Maybe once we have settled status here . . ."

"Even then," she persists, "your family is in Australia. Mine's split across Cyprus, Greece and England. Wherever we are, we can't promise that we won't be needed elsewhere. At some point we'll have ageing parents, or something." She shakes her head.

He runs his hands through his hair. "So, that idea is less feasible than we thought."

"Sounds like it," she says.

The rain beats on in a steady rhythm.

"What would it look like, then? If we went with this," Giannis says, eyeing Androulla's stomach.

She shields it in a gesture that feels overprotective for someone who has yet to make a decision, then drops her arms. "I don't know. I guess . . ."

"You work from home with no set hours. That's one positive," Giannis says, sticking his thumb out. "Your relatives are around, so we'd rarely have to pay for childcare."

"That's true," Androulla says.

He extends his forefinger. "You've never slept well anyway."

She smiles.

"And we don't get out much, so we wouldn't be missing some great party scene all of a sudden."

"No. I feel like we've done that stuff now," she agrees, touching her neck.

"Honestly, all I want is for us to be together," Giannis says. "I don't even think it would matter if we raised a kid without any money. It would grow up with so much love in our little home, our little family."

His face shines through her tears.

"I think so too," she says.

Their kiss is wet and tastes of salt.

"But we're not secure in our home," Androulla remembers, pulling away. She catches sight of the black mould in the shower that will not recede, no matter how hard she scrubs at it. "We're both working illegally. Kostas has managed to get my documents into Immigration, but they're still waiting for approval. I could be deported if Ms Xenofontos doesn't renew my visa. And even if she does, what'll happen next year? I won't be able to apply again, will I? As a dependant with a dependant. She'll kick me out."

"Not if you renew your Greek passport," Giannis says, softly.

"And give up on getting a Cypriot one?" Androulla stares at him.

"You'll get citizenship eventually."

"By time-spent," she says, "not descendancy. If I give up on this process now, I won't be able to start it again. I won't be a real Cypriot, ever."

"Well, no. Neither will I, by your standards," Giannis says.

"But it's different for you."

"Just remind me," he frowns, "why is that again?"

Shifting her weight onto her back foot, Androulla says, "Because you're blood-Cypriot. It doesn't matter how long ago your family emigrated, every generation has married into another Australian-Cypriot family. No one questions your connection to this country, even though it's less immediate than mine."

He bristles.

"I'm not saying it's less meaningful," Androulla says, before he can stop her, "but your great, great grandparents were here. Right? And they left."

"Yeah," Giannis says.

Now Androulla counts on her fingers. "My grandparents, aunts, uncles and cousins are here. I've never thought of them as step-relatives, you know that. But every time someone reminds me that I'm not 'really' Cypriot, it's like they're saying I'm not 'really' part of the family. And that hurts, when I've never felt part of my dad's family either. My 'real' dad," she adds, with air quotes. "This country means everything to me. Clearly, I've given everything to be here."

Giannis's eyes fall once again to her stomach. He lets out a long breath. "I guess that's what you have to decide, then," he says, in a voice that sounds like it is shrivelling up. "What matters more, your place as a daughter or as a mother?"

THE SEVENTEENTH

KOSTAS AND OLYMPIA LIVE in Aglantzia, a municipality reached by turning off of the Limassol Road before it surges into a highway. Their house is in hiding, Olympia has taken to saying, inside what looks like a plain apartment building.

Giannis parks a little way down the road, broad and studded with olive trees.

"Ready?" he asks.

Androulla stares at the fruit, left to rot on the branches.

"As I'll ever be," she says.

They walk hand-in-hand towards the yellowing building, past 'beware of dog' signs and a single swing on an unpaved plot. It creaks in the breeze.

"It's quiet," Androulla says.

"Mmn."

"Cloudy."

"Yeah," Giannis agrees, before looking up.

She leads him down a narrow passage between the building and her parents' Ford Focus. Beyond a stiffened gate, a peeling white staircase winds up to the first floor. The door at the top is shut. Androulla rounds the corner to her parents' garden.

"*Kaliméra*," Olympia greets them, through a glass door. "Come in."

With a glance at the frosted vegetable patch and coiled green hosepipe, Androulla steps inside. Giannis follows her, sliding the door shut behind him. Despite its open-plan, this house is warmer than their apartment. The ceiling is high, so the air conditioner doesn't blow as stiflingly into Androulla's face. She inhales. As always, there is the smell of pastry baking. A hardwood floor, tempered with soft lighting and furnishings in every corner.

"How are you, *paidiá*?" Olympia asks, taking their coats.

Androulla draws inwards as she parts with hers, clasping her elbows in opposite hands. "Yeah, okay. How are you? Can we sit?"

Blinking, her mother indicates a low sofa. "Yes. I'll bring the coffee down."

It is only as her heel disappears up the final step to the kitchen that Androulla thinks of offering to help. Passing the sofa, she takes a straight-backed seat at the table. Giannis sits down beside her.

"One of your *mamá*'s," he says, pointing.

She looks to a cookbook laid out like a centrepiece. Beneath the title *Recipes from Rhodes*, a young Olympia wears a proud smile. On the cover of a second book, *Tales from our Taverna*, she poses in front of her parents' harbour-side restaurant. The restaurant from which holidaymaker Gary Dixon plucked her, thus ending her career as a seasonal waitress and making possible one where she could sell her homesickness, packaged as summer holiday nostalgia, to Britons who fancied themselves above battered fish. Then Gary left her, a new mother and a waitress again, in dreary London, studying Food, Culture and Identity by night. Now, she devises restaurant menus and makes the odd appearance on a low-budget cooking show.

Androulla bites her thumbnail. Perhaps Olympia would have carried on in London, writing bolder and better-selling Greek cookbooks, if she hadn't become a mother. Perhaps Androulla, too, will cease to have time for her writing, if she chooses a child over that pursuit and her love of her country. Overhead, china clinks.

"Are you okay?" Giannis asks, squeezing her hand.

Androulla nods, squeezing back, but does not say a word.

Her parents come down together, with a pot of coffee and a plate of nutty, Christmas-spiced pastries.

"*Takakia*," Olympia says, "fresh from the oven."

"These smell great," Giannis says, taking one.

Kostas passes cups and plates around the table. "*Óla kalá?*" he asks.

"Well, we have some news," Androulla says, waving away a honey-glazed offering.

Kostas tucks in his chair.

"I'm pregnant."

His eyes widen.

"Oh," Olympia breathes. She pushes back from the table, as though to come around and embrace Androulla.

"We don't know what we're going to do yet," Androulla warns, stopping her still, "because obviously, with my status . . . Sorry." She bows her head into her hands.

Giannis's arm warms her shoulders. She feels the vibration as he clears his throat, then a stiffness. Peering through her fingers, she sees her parents staring and tucks her hair back.

"What do you mean, your status?" her stepfather asks.

"I'm a dependant," she sniffs. "I can't be a dependant with a dependant, can I? That doesn't make sense. They won't let me stay."

"Possibly not, on your current visa," Olympia says, glancing at Giannis.

Androulla knows what they are thinking, the pair of them. She grits her teeth. "I still want to be Cypriot."

"You can," Kostas says, pushing his plate to one side. "They won't discriminate against you because you're a mother."

"Are you sure?" Olympia asks him.

"One-hundred percent. They can't," he says.

"So, I could do both?" Androulla repeats. "Have this baby and get my passport? Through descendancy," she clarifies.

A weight lifts its heels from her shoulders, then leaps off entirely as Kostas says yes, she could.

"Will you?" Olympia asks.

Androulla looks to Giannis. His eyes are wide, his shadow overgrown as though stretching towards nightfall.

"I think . . ."

He grips her hand tighter, nodding.

"Yes. I think we will," she says.

Shunting her chair back, Olympia envelops Androulla, then Giannis in her jasmine scent. Kostas comes after her, congratulating them both.

"Sophie?" he smiles.

Recalling his old love for this name, Androulla laughs. He used to crouch on the floor and insist that she give it to one toy in all her games.

"I don't know about Sophie," she says, shaking her head.

She sees Olympia look away and wonders, for the first time, whether her parents discussed the name, too.

"You'll make it work, we all do. I'm happy for you," Olympia imparts, pearly-eyed.

It is raining when Androulla and Giannis depart, thick drops that fall sparsely, as though challenging them to dodge out the way. They play along, half-skipping and sinking breathless into their car. They look at each other. Leaning over the gearstick, Giannis crushes his lips into Androulla's. She tastes the cinnamon on his tongue and scratches her chin raw with his stubble.

"Are you happy?" he asks, cupping her face.

"I think so," she says, reopening her eyes. "Are you? Sure you want this?"

"I am." Giannis sits back. "More than I felt I could tell you before," he says, starting the car.

The rain pokes at the windows as they pick up speed. Androulla watches it, streaking downwards from fine points.

"But this should be a shared decision," she says.

Giannis's eyes remain fixed upon the road. "I wanted it before you were pregnant, I mean. Before we knew that you could be. I didn't want to upset you by saying."

She strokes the hair above his ear.

By the time they arrive home, the rain has picked up. Its distant clamouring adds an air of cosiness to the living room, in which Androulla is curled up with a blanket when Giannis brings her tea. A caffeine-free one, he has made sure, after the non-starter of coffee at her parents'. He places it down on the bookshelf.

"What are you looking at?" he asks.

"Names," Androulla says, turning her phone around to show him.

He rolls his eyes. "Week three?"

"Come on," she says, lifting the blanket to allow him in. "Quick."

"'Unique Baby Names'," Giannis reads, snuggling up next to her. He sneers, "Linus?"

"Charlie Brown's friend," Androulla defends the name, half-heartedly.

"Right. I can see I'm going to have to get involved here," Giannis says.

She laughs, leaning into him, and he kisses her forehead.

"Now?" she says, when he takes out his phone. Then, "Oh."

She watches him filter his property search to two-bed rentals in Nicosia, then sort the results from lowest-to-highest price. The splendour of the first listing makes her catch her breath, before she sees that it is 'sponsored' and four-thousand euros per month. Giannis looks sideways at her, scrolling past it. Androulla nudges him, softly. Their shoulders stiffen in unison. The cheapest apartments are in dank buildings in old town, or well out into the suburbs, and still more expensive than where they live now. Bills not included.

"I don't think we need to worry about moving yet," Androulla says, in a voice high with feigned nonchalance. "We're not having this baby for another nine months. And it won't need its own room straight away, will it?"

Giannis exhales through his teeth. "I guess not, until it's a little older. We could have the money from your book by then," he says, locking his phone.

"I don't know about that book," she reminds him.

"Another one, then. You have time."

She kisses him. "How about literary names? I bet someone's made a list."

She is reaching for her phone again when Giannis remembers his shift at the bar. With a groan, he hoists himself up.

"You look at those and drink your tea. Here, it's probably cold now," he says, handing it to her.

"Thanks." She takes a sip of the lukewarm liquid and tilts her head from side to side.

Giannis gazes at her. "I don't want to leave you. Both," he adds, bending to touch her stomach.

His hand leaves an impression and Androulla holds hers in its place once she is alone, lying on the sofa aglow, shifting to her feet aglow, drifting into the bathroom . . . She stops. The silence resounds. Her stomach is flat, freer of any loose skin or stretch marks than she has ever given it credit for. But it won't be for long, perhaps not ever again. As if to confirm this, it rumbles. Androulla watches her hand drop in the harshly lit mirror. Skipping meals cannot be an option now that there is a mouth to feed, forming inside her. She has slipped back into doing enough of that, she fears, in recent weeks.

Wrapping up on the sofa again, she puts aside the list that she has started with 'Matilda', 'Scout' and 'Jay'. With the rain pounding on beyond the darkened windows, Androulla reads up on preventative bio-oils and what to eat while pregnant. Almost triple what she has been each day, calorie-wise. The thought turns her stomach, and yet she must make it habitable for her miracle child. She can mitigate the effects on her figure, she reads, with gentle walks and yoga.

The Twenty-Third

Androulla squints at her assignment until the throbbing spreads from her head to her temples, and then to her eyes. She presses them shut, digs her fingertips into their lids and reopens them, regretting it. The light from her laptop is splitting. Pushing it shut, she stumbles from her living room.

Her bedroom blinds are down, despite the daylight coming in underneath them. Androulla wrenches both pulls so that their bottom weights crack over the window frames, casting the room into a greyer light. She falls into bed, closing her eyes. The march across her skull goes on. Androulla can feel the points where all her teeth connect to her jawbone. She tries clenching and releasing it, lying on her back and on her side. There is a searing sound, like the threat of a chainsaw above its motor. Rain, she realises, lying back. With a groan, she pulls the duvet over her head.

In the five days since she has been having these migraines, she hasn't taken a painkiller. Giannis's mother says it could hurt the baby, and that Androulla should see a doctor before trusting the word of any pill packet. Her Aunt Chrystalla recommended a gynaecologist when Olympia could not wait to boast. Since then it has been announced that cousin Christina is pregnant, too. And that they should go to prenatal classes together.

Androulla cradles her stomach. Already, she feels an urge to protect her child from premature experiences such as she had with Oscar, and to bless them with ultimate bonds such as she forged with Naomi. She understands that her choices will alter someone else's life, not just her own. For now because she is carrying that person inside her. Later because she will be carrying them with her, through each fraught mealtime and every fracas at Immigration. Her eyelids feel thin.

She has felt nauseous, the last few mornings. But she hasn't been sick. She could take comfort in that, she thought, until Giannis's mother said what a good sign it was to vomit. Vomiting shows that the stomach is churning with pregnancy hormones. Since hearing this, Androulla has wanted nothing more than to be sick. Except, perhaps, to stop feeling green-tinged and as though the palest sliver of light could cleave her skull. To stop this madness altogether.

She hugs her child tighter. When do they develop ears? She imagines her most terrible thoughts echoing down the halls of her body to its nursery, and wants to drown them out with a music box. To install a nightlight and hang a mobile. She wants to be hospitable, and yet not to inhabit herself.

She wills February and her first doctor's appointment to come sooner. This gynaecologist is worth the wait, apparently, one of the best in Cyprus. He will tell her how to manage the internal effects of the pregnancy. And the external ones, Androulla hopes, if she can explain that her body confidence has higher stakes than other women's. That if she slips back into valuing herself solely on physical attractiveness, and feels less attractive, it could wreak havoc. There must be something he can give her, some insider tactic she can use to keep her skin smooth, not taut anywhere but her stomach. She has seen pictures of celebrities with perfect bumps and pencil legs. How do they do it?

The pain in her head is drum-banging, her duvet powerless to drown out the rain. Androulla curls up in the foetal position, like an outermost Russian doll. For the last week, she has eaten well. Brown rice, legumes and lots of dark, leafy greens. Her mother has come by with things like Marmite and salmon that Androulla cannot spend out on, but that she has read are good for the baby. She is still fixated on what she eats, how much of it and when. But if she can shift that fixation onto what she is doing for her child, rather than to her figure, she thinks she can harness it. Just for nine months. And then she can go back to starving herself, she reasons, if that is what she needs to feel sane.

The rain picks up, causing sparks behind her eyes, and Androulla squeezes them tighter. Tears trickle over her nose and pool inside her ear. She is sure she has heard about orgasms for migraines, that arousing yourself is the last thing you might think of in pain, but the best you can do to assuage it. She tries, but her skull shrieks and she feels unworthy. She burrows deeper into her bedding.

When she reopens her eyes, it is to soft lamplight. Her instinct is to shield them, but it no longer hurts to look around. There is only the ghost of the pounding in her head, making it feel hollow and faintly sore as she turns onto her other ear. Giannis is climbing into bed beside her, weighing upon the mattress.

"Hey," he starts. "Is that too bright? Do you want it off?"

He reaches for the light switch, rocking the bed. Androulla groans and paws at his chest. In the darkness, he shifts closer. He smells fresh from the shower, and she feels conscious of her clammy skin as he wraps his arms around her.

"Sorry I woke you," he murmurs.

She shakes her head. "What time is it? Have you been at work?"

"Uni," he says. "It's just after ten."

She counts her lost hours until they rack up and elude her again. "Mmn."

"Was your head hurting?" Giannis asks.

"It's been so bad," she says, in a frayed voice.

"Oh, Wife." He kisses her hairline.

"Sorry, I'm disgusting," she mumbles.

"You're perfect." He kisses her again.

She rolls onto her back, sending another distant pang through her head. The rain is gentler now, blanketing the expanse tramped down by her headache with a softness like snow.

"Hey, Wife?" she says. "I've been feeling kind of put off by something."

"What's that?" Giannis asks, turning onto his elbow.

Androulla takes a breath. "I've always thought of myself as fairly intuitive. I don't know if you'd agree."

"Yeah. For the most part I'd say so," Giannis says.

"So, I've been waiting to get a sense of the baby's gender." She stares upwards, and the ceiling becomes no more visible. "I just don't have a clue, and it's inside me. I thought I'd have a stronger connection to it."

"You're too hard on yourself," Giannis says, with a head-shake that disrupts their bedding. "It's so early on. And gender doesn't mean anything, anyway. You know that."

Androulla sighs. "Yeah."

"Let's get some sleep," he says, throwing his arm over her again.

The rain sounds louder for their stillness.

Sightlessly, Androulla blinks. "Gianni?"

"Mmn."

"Will you still be attracted to me, after this?"

Moving his head onto her pillow, he kisses her cheek. "You know I will. Always," he says.

She is sure he means this. And yet she drifts away from him, into a subconscious conflation of what she should be putting into her body with what she should be putting onto it. She is heavily pregnant in the dream, with her stomach rounding away from her. It will return to its resting flatness, she is soothing herself, less like a balloon deflating and more like an elastic band pinging back because she is doing everything right. Running her hands over her bump to coat it, lovingly, in Marmite. She starts around her belly button and works her way out, until her whole body is smeared into obscurity. Her only remaining, distinguishing feature is her motherhood.

She wakes up breathless.

THE TWENTY-FIFTH

"*Gelá sas*," ANDROULLA SAYS, poking her head around the door marked 'Biometrics'.

She has waited outside for half an hour, watching the red numbers on a black screen tick up through the six-hundreds. Several of the chairs around her are taken by people worrying raffle-like tickets between their fingers and thumbs. But none of them have responded when, every few minutes, the number has jumped up by six or eight.

"*Chaírete*," says the heavyset woman, alone in the room. She has glasses, two screen monitors and a Perspex window guarding her smile.

Gingerly, Androulla steps towards her. "Erm, I have this . . ."

The woman pulls the signed receipt under her window. "Okay," she says, adding it to a pile upon her desk. "Sit."

Androulla follows her gesture to a chair on the opposite wall. She looks to the woman for further guidance, lowering her tote bag to the floor when none comes. The woman scrawls, audibly, across a page. Her touch depresses her keyboard and then her mouse with a series of 'click's. Androulla watches her flyaway hairs over the top of her screen. The room around them is white, rectangular and as clinical-smelling as the rest of the Migration Department, except with a lower ceiling. Under the glare of a camera, her skin prickles.

"Look up," the woman instructs her.

The lens slides in and out, whirring, while the woman remains seated. Androulla tries not to think that it can see through her. She tries to focus on how uncomfortable she is having her picture taken, rather than on the fact that she will not be in the picture alone. Her heart flips. Whether or not it is visible to the naked eye, Androulla is posing 'with child'. The forms she signed weeks ago, declaring her single and without dependants, are outdated. But they have been approved. With days to spare, she has been granted a year's extension to her stay in Cyprus.

"Okay," the woman says.

Androulla lifts up her bag.

"Put your index finger here." The woman points to a scanner on the edge of her desk.

A red light appears in the window beneath Androulla's fingertip, copying her print that does not resemble Kostas's. It will look closer to her own child's, who will never in their life have to fight for this family or homeland. They will have a Cypriot passport from the day they are born, Androulla imagines. Already, her chest feels swollen with envy and delight.

"Other finger," the woman prompts her.

When it is done, she tells Androulla that her new visa should be ready in three-to-four months. Not only is Androulla free to remain in the country, she cannot leave until she has the card.

"Thank you," she smiles, as she leaves Biometrics.

The people waiting stare blankly as she floats past them, down one ramp and up another to the building's back doors. She emerges blinking, as though from a daytime film screening. Was it raining before she went in? With her head bowed to the icy droplets, she stalks past the security guards.

"*Geiá sou, kopèla*," one of them calls, as she reaches the gate.

On the other side, there are cold-pinched lips and hungry eyes. Knowing that she might never again pass through on the grounds that she did today, Androulla looks back at the guard. Her smile is both smug and scarce, for the secret that she carries inside her. The gate clanks shut on her heels.

Giannis is in the shower when she arrives home, readying himself for work. The sound of droplets raining down is more acute than it was outside, and accompanied by a clean scent.

"Nice and warm in here," Androulla says, slipping into the bathroom.

He inhales through his teeth, his eyes fixed to the open door. "It was . . ."

She closes it.

"How was that, then?" he asks.

"Good." Intending to beat any migraines to bed in an orderly manner, Androulla takes out a makeup wipe. "It's funny, having the photo and stuff done for my new card, and knowing I'll look back and say, 'I was pregnant in that'. You know?"

"Yeah." Eyes scrunched, Giannis tips his head back and the shampoo foams down his back. "Are you happy, though? To have secured another year."

"I'm excited about what it means for the baby," Androulla says, dragging the heel of her hand across the mirror.

A break appears in the condensation and she bends to see her mascara come off. Even as the water stops in the shower, it carries on beyond the window.

"That's great," Giannis says, his voice taking on an echo. "So, last night. Imran had a run in with this table of Russian guys . . ."

Androulla blinks. More steam has settled upon the mirror, blinding her to her progress. She wipes it away.

"There were loads of them," Giannis says, "sat around the pool table. They all ordered beer, so Imran had to take this tray of, I swear, about twelve pints over. Anyway. One guy thought he'd be helpful, and lifted a pint off the tray. And you're not supposed to do that."

Androulla sees her husband stop drying, as if for emphasis, before the mirror fogs up again.

"You're supposed to let the runners take the drinks off themselves," he goes on. "Otherwise you can unbalance the tray, and–"

"Sorry." She faces him, shaking her head. "What?"

Giannis stands upright, pulling the towel from his hair. "Basically, this guy took a drink off of Imran's tray, and he spilled the whole lot over the pool table."

"Yeah, no. I get that," Androulla says, lowering her make-up wipe. "I just don't understand how we got there. I feel like we were talking about the baby, and suddenly we're on beer."

There is a strangeness to Giannis's smile as he hangs his towel back. "Okay, sorry. Just thought I'd tell you the latest."

"I do want to hear it," Androulla assures him.

But she cannot follow his leap from their child to his colleague, cannot forgo thinking about their child for anything. Not even for a moment, she realises, as her section of mirror clouds over again. With a short breath out, Giannis shoots into their bedroom for his clothes, leaving Androulla in the swirling mist.

She tries to work on the sofa when he leaves, her laptop piled on top of her with the cushions. She tries to focus on the restructuring of a cookbook that someone has written with their ageing grandmother, and to persuade them that 'ageing' is a needless additive to 'grandmother'. Meanwhile, all she can think about is her own grandmother, who had her mother, who had her, and the kind of mother that she will be. Androulla fails to grasp it. How can Giannis think about anything else?

Lifting her phone, she addresses this question to the last person she might have expected. His voice sounds in her ear before she can think better of it, and she dives straight in off the board of his niceties.

"What were you like? When *Mamá* was pregnant."

"Oh," her father says. "Well, how do you mean?"

"Like, could you focus on other things?" Androulla asks. "When you knew there was a whole life forming inside you guys, that you were about to be responsible for. Did you have the brain space?"

"Erm."

She should have known this would be too graphic a question for Gary. Hearing the discomfort in his silence, Androulla wishes she hadn't called.

"I think I did, actually," he says. Then, "Hello?"

"Yeah, I'm here," she says. "Right."

Because of course her father had brain space. He had nothing but space from Olympia when she was pregnant, fearing that he had shut himself in a room with the wrong woman and she had locked it. He broke out in a panic.

Androulla cradles her stomach. More than ever, she struggles to fathom, "How could you leave? When your baby was there."

"Well," he sighs. "You were and you weren't there, at that point. It's different for men."

"How?"

"What?"

"How is it different?" Androulla asks him.

The rain is still coming down outside, reinforcing the air of dampness from the bathroom.

"It's different, in that . . ." Gary pauses. "What you said before, about a life forming inside 'us', was inaccurate, really. Wasn't it?"

Androulla's laptop falls into shade.

"You can be as involved as you like as a dad," Gary says. "But until your child is in front of you, until you can see it and touch it, you can pretty much compartmentalise it."

"But I can't see or touch it, as a woman," Androulla says, wriggling her mouse.

"No. But you can feel it, I suppose. And you have to think of it constantly, don't you, with what you're eating and drinking? Unless you want it to come out a bit strange."

"Dad!" she scolds.

"Oh, you know what I mean," he says. "You develop a bond from the start."

"And you don't," she repeats.

"Not in the same way," he admits.

With a dull thud, she closes her laptop.

"Our bond comes later, in a rush at the birth. The enormity of it sinks in. And it never diminishes, that feeling. From any distance," he says, with more meaning than she has heard him say anything. "Andy, are you . . ?"

A single tear streaks over her smile. "Yes."

THE TWENTY-EIGHTH

IT IS BY CHANCE that Androulla hears the Frenchwoman talking up her book on glucose spikes. The symptoms of constant hunger, chronic fatigue and hot flushes. The development of conditions such as diabetes, cancer and PCOS. Androulla blinks. The woman says it again. Scientists have discovered a significant link between high insulin levels and the infertility caused by polycystic ovary syndrome.

Snatching her phone off the kitchen counter, Androulla checks the podcast that is playing off the back of the one she has just finished. A steady rain is falling outside, filling her ears with its pulse. Turning her phone up to full volume, she resumes spooning Greek yoghurt into a breakfast bowl. The tub feels colder in her palm.

PCOS is a disease caused by too much insulin. Insulin tells the ovaries to produce more testosterone, in some cases causing acne, missed periods and extra body hair, the Frenchwoman explains. The more glucose spikes in our diet, the higher our insulin levels. Therefore, the higher our risk of infertility.

The host of the podcast cites a friend with PCOS, who used to struggle with binge-eating. Could there be a link there?

Androulla drops her spoon and its clattering rings through her ears. Even as she stops it, the suggestion haunts her. That her skipped breakfasts and discarded lunches, her walks home from school as an empty child – who knew no better than to wage this war on herself – could have led from her gorges on peanut butter cups, to spikes in her glucose levels. From too much insulin, to excess testosterone. And an inability to conceive children of her own one day. She fits the lid back onto the yoghurt pot.

By keeping their glucose levels under control, the French-woman has seen PCOS-sufferers reduce their symptoms. Some who were infertile for years have gone on to conceive, she says, by eating in a way that prevents peaks and crashes. Androulla's eyes go to her smoothie maker. In an effort to regain control over her disordered eating, she spent the autumn on a regimen of spinach for breakfast and berries for lunch, with snacks of raw nuts and plant-based dinners at five p.m. She reintroduced exercise and stopped drinking alcohol. A breath of laughter escapes her. Before she had heard of this woman, Androulla was following her instructions. Priming her body for pregnancy, she realises, without the faintest idea that it was possible.

Returning the yoghurt to the fridge, she feels a rush of cold. Then another as the Frenchwoman speaks of the dissociation that led to her studies. Her descriptions of feeling disconnected from reality, of looking at her hands and thinking that they didn't feel like hers, strike Androulla. She stares out at the rain and recalls her job of blue-skying house photos, the six-week period in which she sat unresponsive at her desk. The months last summer – beneath a real blue sky – when she forgot her concerns about personal safety, and her compassion for the love of her life. Remorse turns her stomach. And yet it is true, her detachment lifted when she began eating again. She picks up her spoon.

While she finishes her breakfast, Androulla opens the app for expectant mothers that she has just downloaded. Its addition looks wholesome, out of keeping with the AA and SAA icons still on her home screen. It informs her that at five weeks, her baby will be the size of an orange seed. At six weeks, a sweet pea. For the first time that she can recall, her full stomach makes her smile.

FEBRUARY

THE FIFTH

RAIN DRUBS AT THE window as Androulla climbs onto the examination table. It runs the length of a room in a Strovolos clinic, between a bookshop abandoned years ago and one that she frequents now.

"Lay back," the gynaecologist says, raising his transducer. "I want to see your belly."

Androulla draws her knees up, careful not to disturb the paper towel, and tucks her jumper over her bra. Upturning what looks like a PVA glue bottle, Doctor Constantinou cools her stomach. She giggles.

"Relax your muscles," he smiles, nosing the gel around.

She follows his gaze to the grey machine, echoing her insides on a mounted screen. As she watches it, the gynaecologist digs deeper into her abdomen. Her bladder sings.

"Okay," he says, retracting the transducer.

By the time she looks up again, the screen is blank.

"It's a bit small to see anything with the external one," Doctor Constantinou says, pulling on a plastic glove. "Let's try with the internal."

"Okay," Androulla says.

The transducer rocks as he hangs it up. There is the sound of a drawer sliding open, followed by a short rip. She sits up on her elbows as he pulls a condom from its wrapper.

"Lay back," he instructs her, in his same calm voice. "Open your legs."

He stretches the rubber over a white, phallic implement. Letting her knees fall open, Androulla remembers her husband in the adjoining room. He is sitting in a chair at the gynaecologist's desk, watching her with wide eyes. She motions for him to turn away, horror startling her as it appears to paralyse him.

"Don't look," she mouths.

Doctor Constantinou follows her gaze. "Shall we close this?" he asks, pulling a curtain across.

"Thank you." Androulla drops her head back to the table.

She catches her breath. The gynaecologist is inside her, staring at the screen while she folds her lips inwards and they agree, without words, that this is not a sexual encounter. Even if it is penetrative and feels disconcertingly good.

"There," he says, stilling his hand. "You see?"

Androulla cranes up at the screen. She sees the tunnel where the probe is opening out into a cavern, its walls bleeding from grey to black. And there, hugging one side–

"The embryo."

A breath of laughter escapes her. Doctor Constantinou leans to turn a knob on the machine. There is a sound like crickets, and then a throbbing.

"Is that . . ?" she starts.

"The heartbeat," he confirms.

The sound fills the room, obscuring the rain. Androulla's eardrums ignite. This pulse, she realises, is the beat to which she will march. It will inflate her body with purpose, and deliver into a greater love than she might ever have known. With her eyes on the screen, she caresses her stomach.

"When did you say your last period was?" the gynaecologist asks.

"In November?" she answers, vaguely.

"November," he repeats. "Are you sure?"

"I think so," she manages, as he probes deeper inside her.

"But you have irregular periods?"

"Sometimes."

He pulls back, stealing her baby away from the screen. "Okay."

Androulla watches him throw the condom into a corner bin, with twin pangs in her chest and groin. She lifts her hands off her stomach, slick.

"Between the date of your last period and the size of the embryo, we'll call it six-and-a-half weeks," Doctor Constantinou says. He holds out a wad of translucent paper.

Drying herself, Androulla pulls up her jeans and follows him around the curtain. She feels in need of a shower, though she smells chemically clean from the gel. In the office next door, Giannis is slumped deep in his chair. He looks up with an awed expression, as though his ears, too, are still ringing with their baby's heartbeat. Androulla takes the seat next to him, a smile bulging from her eyes.

"*Loipón*," the gynaecologist says, sliding a fold of paper across his desk. "This is your scan."

They surge forwards at once, poring over the image. Their baby an oval of grey, with a flash of white through its centre. Its spirit, Androulla thinks, tracing the flames of its heartbeat along a straight line. Giannis looks at her with so much gratitude that her vision blurs.

"Everything looks healthy, the heartbeat is strong for this age. It's remarkable, actually," Doctor Constantinou says, staring after the sonogram. "Although it is small, so we'll keep an eye on that." He pulls his notepad towards him. "I'm going to write you some folic acid, some multivitamins. You can get those from the pharmacy next door. You know that your womb has some scarring from a previous rupture," he says, uncapping his pen.

"Yes," Androulla concedes.

He nods. "The first trimester is delicate anyway. But you," he tells her, "should be very careful. No unhealthy foods, no exercise except for walking–"

Giannis takes her hand.

"–no housework or heavy lifting. No sex for another six weeks."

His grip turns limp.

Androulla raises her eyebrows. "Would it be bad, if we had been . . ?"

"You'll stop now," the gynaecologist says, with a wave of his hand.

"I've also been having some migraines . . ."

"Paracetamol is fine," he declares. He signs off on his notepad with a stamp and holds the page out to her. "I want to see you again in two weeks, to see how the pregnancy is going on. Okay? You can make an appointment with my secretary on your way out."

"*Efcharistó pára, pára polý,*" Giannis thanks him.

Outside, Androulla feels numb to the rain. Like she has transcended the clouds and is floating on a plain high above them, even as her husband holds her to earth by the hand.

"It's a boy," she tells him, when night falls.

"How do you know?" he asks her.

"I just do," she says.

For it was like their baby was speaking to her, winking and pulsing in Morse code as the gynaecologist probed around, the light shifted and the heart beat. Androulla saw visions of the future like memories already made, upon that screen. She saw herself smiling. Saw a child of two or three climbing onto her husband's lap, a book with a great blue whale on the cover waving from his hand. Her steadily-grown love for the child showing upon Giannis's face, all at once. Their son is alive. They are burying their faces into his neck and breathing his warmth and bearing him up, shrieking with laughter, while the Mediterranean Sea crashes around them. Their son is alive, and his name is Jonah. In her dreams, Androulla calls it again and again until he responds.

The Seventh

Androulla's underwear sticks as she pulls it down, just briefly. She looks. There, in the crotch of her thong, is the fluid. It has the colour and consistency of spit in the sink after coffee, except that there is no water with which to wash it away.

Legs trembling, she sinks the rest of the way down onto the toilet. Her thong gets caught in her toes and she shakes it out, releasing her bladder. In the last two weeks, she has had to make copious trips to the bathroom. But only in the last two days have those trips turned fraught. Reaching for her phone, she types 'is it' into Google and selects her previous search of 'normal to bleed while pregnant'. The screen turns white. She watches a blue line struggle across it, holding her breath.

Apparently, up to one in four women experiences some spotting during their pregnancy. This doesn't always mean there is a problem. But it can be a sign.

263

Dabbing between her legs, Androulla braces herself to see blood on the toilet paper. Spotting, she thinks. And yet her eyes slide back to her stained thong.

Her laptop is on the sofa where she left it, under doctors' orders to rest. She saves the horticultural piece that she has been writing on her back and shuts it down. Then she looks up the number of Doctor Constantinou's clinic. She perches on the edge of the sofa while her phone rings, until the receiver 'click's and she starts to her feet again.

"*Kaliméra*," she greets his secretary. "I came in for an ultrasound on Monday, my name is Androulla Dixon. Demetriou," she corrects herself, blinking. "I don't know if you remember me . . ."

"Yes?" the girl says.

Androulla holds her eyes shut. "I've been having some bleeding, since then."

"You're bleeding now?" the girl repeats. "Since Monday?"

"Not bleeding, bleeding," Androulla says, at the alarm in her voice. She returns to the assurance of, "Spotting, I think. On toilet paper. And just now in my underwear." When she reopens her eyes, the world looks blurry. "I was hoping I could see the doctor again, or at least speak to him?"

"Yes, come now," the girl bids her.

"Now?"

"As soon as you can," she urges.

Androulla is shaky behind the wheel, missing when she goes to set her indicator and gasping when the first drop of rain hits her windscreen. She parks across the road from the clinic and catches her breath. She crosses the threshold moments later, dripping wet and expectant of a scolding. She feels young enough, suddenly. Too young.

Inside, three secretaries sit behind a wall of Perspex screens. The one whose voice Androulla recognises, heavily made-up behind wide-framed glasses, points her to a seat on its own, facing the rest of the waiting room that is set up like a London tube. Androulla fidgets. Scratchy blue fabric lines the chairs. A chemical scent taints the air. Wide-eyed babies plaster the walls, selling Pampers and Huggies with toothless smiles. Androulla lowers her gaze.

The door marked 'Doctor Constantinou' swings open, emitting a woman with her stomach distended and her eyes set on some shining future. At a nod from the secretary, Androulla crosses the coconut stream left in her wake.

"*Kýrios* Constantinou?" she says.

"Androulla." The gynaecologist beckons her into his office, shutting his desk drawer as she does the door. "My secretary tells me you've had some bleeding."

"Yes," she says, taking her bag off her shoulder.

Before she can sit down, he points her to the examination table in the adjoining room. "Lay down, please. I want to see your belly."

There is no giggling this time, as he rubs the gel around her stomach. The cold is permeating, the transducer a dead weight.

"Okay," Doctor Constantinou says.

Androulla looks sideways at him.

"The sack is intact. You see? Here."

She doesn't realise until she follows his finger to the screen that she has been avoiding it. Protecting herself from the sight of a grey abyss, echoing louder for its loss. But there he is, still swaddled inside her. Jonah. Her heart lifts.

"The heartbeat looks strong," Doctor Constantinou says, pressing the transducer down harder.

Androulla nods, ignoring her bladder's protest.

"What colour has it been? The blood," he asks.

"It's coming out, like, brown? Mostly when I go to the toilet. But I've had some in my underwear today," she admits.

He nods. "Brown is fine. As long as it doesn't turn red, that means it's old blood that your body is expelling, probably from a missed cycle or something like that."

"So, if it does turn red," she says.

"Then we'll talk again." Doctor Constantinou leans towards the screen. "It does look small. Very small," he repeats.

Androulla watches him frown until the weight lifts off her stomach. He hands her some tissue paper.

"I'm going to write you some pills. Hormones," he clarifies, hanging up his transducer, "to help with the growth. Because sometimes, in this state, it can stop."

The room turns cold. With half the gel still coating her stomach, Androulla zips up her jeans.

"I want you to take two of these pills per day, one in the morning and one at night," Doctor Constantinou calls, from his office.

He is jotting this down when she rounds the corner, signing his name in a narrow script.

"Okay," Androulla murmurs, sinking into a seat across his desk.

He caps his pen. "I notice you paid for our last appointment in cash. You're not in GESY?"

"No," she admits. "I'm not a citizen."

He cocks his head. "What do you do for work, Androulla *mou*?"

She is halfway to telling him that she is a writer. The mere ghost of one for now, perhaps, but determined to become more material before the baby arrives and it is too late. She runs out of time to drag her dream into the daylight.

"I don't work," she lies. "But my partner does."

"Your partner is Cypriot, *nai*? Actually, both of you . . ." The gynaecologist's frown deepens.

"Erm, descended from," Androulla says, vaguely.

"Okay. I don't know what your situation is exactly," he concludes, dropping his pen. "But if you can get into the healthcare system, into GESY, do that. Otherwise, the birth will be very dear." He brings his stamp down on the page.

She takes at it. "And these pills . . ."

"Should support the growth of the baby," he says. "We have an appointment in two weeks, *nai*?"

"Yes."

"So we'll do another scan, and hope to see a heartbeat then."

"Right," Androulla says, staring at the sonogram that is folded between them.

He doesn't offer it to her.

Surrendering another thirty euros to his secretary, Androulla leaves the clinic. It doesn't matter that the rain soaks through her jumper and jeans. She is the coat, her skin shrieking like nylon as she shields her son. She drowns it out with the windscreen wipers and drives off at speed.

At home, she kicks off her shoes. Hangs up her keys. Stands in the kitchen, where the smell of last night's dinner is still hanging in the air, and breaks out in tears. She doesn't know what else she can be doing. She is eating more than she has in ten years to support this baby. But she wasn't, comes a voice from the back of her mind. In the early weeks, she was back to one lean meal a day, for the most part. Androulla chokes on an inhalation. That time shouldn't count. She didn't know, it wasn't fair. Since testing positive, she has eaten good, healthy things that she has researched at length. Broccoli for Jonah's bone and tissue development. Salmon for his brain and eye growth.

Yet he looks small, and this is the third day that she has seen blood in her discharge. Despite the gynaecologist's reassurances, it is alarming. Androulla goes to the toilet and holds at the paper between her legs until she turns colour-blind. She flushes it away and strips off her wet clothes. Her skin feels clammy. Last night, she recalls as she enters her bedroom, she told Giannis that she was afraid she could lose their baby. Even as he tried to comfort her, she felt his tears sliding down her neck. Their bed stands unmade.

Just relax, their relatives keep saying. Stress is the worst thing. In clean pyjamas, Androulla lies back on the sofa. But she doesn't know how to be calm.

THE NINTH

LAST NIGHT, THE CRAMPS returned. The ones that came without her period several weeks ago, to warn Androulla of her pregnancy. Their steel plates grind together, sending sparks through her abdomen. She closes her eyes. Inhales the scent from Giannis's pillow. Lets the sound of the rain soothe her, until it nudges her bladder. She eases herself out of bed.

In the bathroom, her breath snares. She almost drops her fold of toilet paper before lifting it up, first to the bare bulb with its withering glare, then to the window and its dreary haze. With a whimper, she steps out into the hallway and turns on the light there. Red. The stain is a shock against the white of the paper. Androulla blinks and sees it on the insides of her eyelids, in place of the sun.

She returns to bed with a sanitary towel, rustling when she rolls onto one side or the other, until she cannot stand it any longer and goes back into the bathroom. She gawks. There is no blood on the towel. And on the toilet paper, the same brown discharge as she has seen before, that Doctor Constantinou has told her not to worry about. Androulla holds her head. The sound of the rain fills her ear canals, bursting their banks and flooding her brain with nonsensical terror. She flounders.

The next time she checks, her blood is brown. Then red again.

She calls Doctor Constantinou's clinic, clinging tight to her phone and spluttering that something is wrong, she needs to be seen again. His secretary puts her on hold. Androulla's urge to pace gives way to pain, and she sinks onto the edge of the sofa.

"Androulla *mou*," his voice sounds, then.

She sits upright.

"If something is going wrong, it will take time to show up on the scan," he says. "We have an appointment in ten days. You'll have to wait until then, okay?"

Her mouth hangs open as she lowers her phone, the after-image of red blood still searing her eyes. Why didn't he sound surprised? She discovers the answer in one search, for the reason why someone might be prescribed the pills that she has taken four of so far. One each morning and another each night, as instructed. This drug is for women with hormone imbalances, Google says, who are at risk of suffering miscarriages.

Another cramp keens in Androulla's abdomen and she curls up, hugging her knees.

"Please," she whispers to her son, with more feeling than she has ever known. "Please stay . . ."

The Tenth

He is leaving her.

Saliva flies out through Androulla's teeth as she understands. She has been holding on with all her might, fists clenched, eyes scrunched as she prayed to a power that she had never believed in. Now she is leaking tears because He is not listening, or because Jonah isn't.

"Stay," Androulla has told her son.

As the day has worn on and her discharge thickened, she has begged him. She feels him wrenching away in her stomach, sliding between her legs, and she knows she has failed. That the most basic part of parenting is having your child at heel, and if she cannot manage that then forget the rest. She was never meant to be a mother.

Dragging her legs off the sofa, Androulla swallows bile. She feels the deluge as she stands, as dizzily as if it is the blood from her head that she is losing. Her gasp resounds through the bathroom. The mess in her underwear is viscid, a bolder red than any that she has seen with a period and more than her sanitary towels can absorb, even as she changes them. The last one comes unstuck and lands, heavily, in the bin. Before its lid clangs shut, the others bray. Androulla has visions of them all riding up on a red tide, spilling over her bare feet and staining their soles so that wherever she goes, for the rest of her life, she will leave a trail of this death. Its odour sends her coughing, covering her mouth and nose with one hand as she tears open a new pad with the other. Not looking down, not wanting to see the water take her son as she empties her bladder. A blade lodges itself in her abdomen and she collapses back onto the sofa.

Her phone buzzes.

Naomi. 'How's it been today? Xx'.

She answers on the first ring.

"I think it's over," Androulla whispers. "I'm losing him."

Naomi sucks the air away from her ear. "How do you know?"

Between sobs, Androulla tells her.

"Wait," Naomi says. Her voice sounds thinner, like she has angled her phone away. "What are those hormones you're on?"

Androulla's snivels fill the silence while they await the results of her internet search.

Then, "Andy!"

She catches her breath. "What is it?"

"'The most commonly reported side effects are nausea, abdominal pains and vaginal haemorrhage'. It's the pills," Naomi reveals.

"Oh my god . . ." Relief washes through Androulla's body, and still the pain racks it. Her smile descends into harder sobbing.

"Oh, Andy," her sister repeats, ceasing her cheers.

"Sorry," she sniffs.

"No, don't apologise. That's a relief, though, isn't it?" Naomi asks, softly.

"I mean, yeah. Of course. But it would have been nice to know," Androulla says, letting her spare hand thud to her side, "that the side effects of my anti-miscarriage pills, could make it look like I was having a miscarriage." She scoffs. "What the fuck?"

"It's like antidepressants causing 'suicidal thoughts'," her sister agrees. "I don't know who designs these things."

She stays on the phone until seven o' clock, when Giannis is due home from his day shift.

"Just choose to believe it's the side effects, however you feel," she advises, as they are saying goodbye. "It'll make the waiting easier until your next scan."

"I love you," Androulla says.

A key turns in the lock. Dropping her phone, she holds her arms out for her husband.

"Hi, Wife," he smiles, shrugging his coat off. "How are you going?"

"Hi, Wife . . ."

He leans to kiss her.

"Oh," she says, as his hair wets her face.

He smells more forest-like even than usual.

"Yeah, sorry," he says. "It's still raining out."

As he stands upright, Androulla hears the downpour outside and remembers the one between her legs. A fresh sheet of pain scrunches itself up inside her and she cries out.

"What's going on?" Giannis's hand is on her shoulder.

"It's fine," she breathes. "I'm fine. It's just these pills, causing some pain . . ."

"Have you spoken to the doctor?" he asks.

She nods, feeling his eyes on her twisting body.

"Have you eaten? Do you want some water?" he persists.

His wedding ring 'clink's against her glass and she grabs his wrist.

"Don't go."

"I'll come back," he assures her. "I'm just going to fill up your water, okay? Why don't you choose something for us to watch together?" He takes the TV remote off the bookshelf and slots it into her hand.

As he turns away, the remote slides from Androulla's grasp. She lets her head roll sideways, shivering hot and sweating cold so that she doesn't know what to say when Giannis comes back and offers her a blanket. He puts her water down on the floor.

"Want to just leave your legs out?" he suggests.

Nodding, Androulla lets him slide his arm around and tuck her shoulders in. His breath catches as he strains to retrieve the remote, without disturbing her.

"What are we going to watch, then?"

She answers into his sweatshirt, taking deep breaths of his eucalyptus scent.

"Hmn?" he murmurs, stroking her hair.

"*The Princess Bride*," she croaks, louder.

His chest sinks away from her ear.

"Right. That old crowd-pleaser," he says, with an audible grin.

Androulla laughs until the pain strikes again at her abdomen. Giannis holds her closer.

The film begins with a man reading to his poorly grandson, and Androulla closes her eyes to recall watching it with her father. To recall his sofa in his living room and his arm draped around her, however limply, when she was a child and not sick with worry about her own. She hears the best lines – 'As you wish', 'You killed my father, prepare to die', 'Inconceivable!' – and feels their charm soften even Giannis. But the pain worsens. As the night darkens, the rain falls harder and the film plays on towards its climax, Androulla writhes. Several times, Giannis asks her if she wants him to turn it off.

"You wish," she manages, between pants.

"As I wish?" he quotes the film.

"Ha." Her mock-laughter gives way to a grimace.

She is damp with sweat when the credits roll, fighting her way out of the blanket and then back underneath it.

"Are you sure this is the pills?" Giannis asks her.

"It must be," she maintains. "The timing of this, after everything looked so good on Monday . . ."

"Have you taken any painkillers? Should I get the Parac-etamol?" he asks.

"I don't know if it's safe, with the hormones," she starts. "Who are you calling?"

"The pharmacy," he says, lifting his phone.

"Aren't they closed?"

"They have an out-of-hours line. *Kalispéra* . . ."

He goes back and forth with the murmur in his ear, while Androulla cradles and clutches her stomach in fraught turns.

"What are those pills called?" Giannis asks her.

She tells him, and he repeats their name to the pharmacist. Then to a second pharmacist when the first says that they cannot advise Androulla. She must speak to her doctor. The second one says the same.

"But that's their job," Androulla cries, "to advise people on this stuff. Isn't it? How am I supposed to get hold of my doctor on a Saturday night?"

The pain courses through her body and she arches, turn-ing onto her side. At a touch to her elbow, she squints upwards. Giannis is holding his phone out to her. As the call time ticks up on the screen, her eyebrows lift. He nods.

Sitting upright, she takes the phone. "Hello?"

"*Kalispéra*," says the midwife, on call overnight at Doctor Constantinou's clinic. She has the smooth, deep voice of someone watching the moon in a cloudless sky. "Are you okay?"

Androulla falters. This question is so out of touch with the stale smell that has festered around her, and with the clinical one she can taste through the phone, that her heart cleaves.

"No. Thank you, erm." Her voice quivers. "I'm pregnant, I'm a patient of Doctor Constantinou's, and he put me on these hormone pills a couple of days ago . . . I'm having some quite severe side effects and I was just wondering if I'd be safe to take Paracetamol."

"Okay. What kind of side effects?" the midwife asks.

"The bleeding," Androulla says, "and the abdominal pains."

Beside her, Giannis shifts.

"Is it a lot of bleeding?" the midwife asks.

Androulla passes her phone between hands. "It has been today, yeah," she admits.

"And whereabouts are the pains?"

"In my abdominals," she repeats, catching Giannis's eye.

He stands up to turn on the light.

"Higher up or lower down?" the midwife asks.

"Lower down, I think," Androulla says, rubbing her stomach. "Like, around where my ovaries are?"

"In that case," the midwife says.

There is a 'ping' as Giannis presses the light switch, and a beat before its signal translates into light. Androulla blinks.

"I'm going to give you *Kýrios* Constantinou's mobile number."

"Why?" she bleats.

"Pains associated with this drug are usually in the upper abdominals. I'm sorry," the midwife says, "but this doesn't sound like something that can wait until the morning." Her voice maintains its smoothness as she reads out the gynaecologist's number, but loses its musing quality. As if the clouds have spread to her patch of sky and she, too, has turned away from her window.

Androulla takes the number down with a trembling hand. "Thank you," she sniffs.

She is pulling away from Giannis before she hangs up, passing his phone back and shutting herself in their bedroom with hers, alone. Her heart beats at her chest. The rain lashes beyond. The dialling tone prods its talons into her ear until Doctor Constantinou picks up. Androulla steadies herself.

She says, "Sorry to disturb you."

She tells him what she told the midwife.

She asks, "What should I do?"

"Stop taking the pills. Everything I gave you," he repeats, "stop it now. You can take whatever painkillers you want, and come to the clinic on Monday morning. First thing, okay? You don't need to make an appointment."

Androulla stares at her unmade bed.

"Androulla *mou*?"

"Yeah," she says, drying her tears.

"Don't try to stop the bleeding, before I see you. You need to empty yourself," Doctor Constantinou warns.

"Okay," she says, knowing that if there were any way to stop it, she would have held on to Jonah. She would have held on until her knuckles broke through her skin. "Thank you," she supposes, and hangs up the phone.

The bedroom door creaks open. Faced with her husband, she bows into her hands. He crushes them as he holds her, and she cannot breathe to tell him. She has been deluding herself. The drugs don't matter, and they clearly don't work. She is losing their baby. As she convulses, her earlier internet searches clatter across her mind.

'How to prevent stretch marks'.

'Dieting during pregnancy'.

'Is sex the same after childbirth'?

A dropdown of vain and indulgent questions, none of which conveyed a shred of her motherly love to the world beyond her jabbing thumbs. The answers no longer matter. She cannot believe they ever did. The states of her skin and of her sex life would have lost their importance, if Jonah had lived. Androulla would have been happy, whatever went on around him. The pain bends her over the bed, with Giannis's hand on her back. They will never know the person that their son would have been. Even if they conceive again, it will be another child with another life course, and they will simply never get to see Jonah's.

Androulla cannot account for the noise that rips from her lungs. It is animal, the wail of a mother losing a child. Her skin feels as raw as if she is standing out in the rain, for her grief. But there is nothing to attach it to, no body to bury and no photos to reminisce over with her friends or extended family. Most of them don't know Jonah existed, let alone that he is ceasing to. There will be no ceremony, no memorial, no stone to touch or return to in the long, barren winters that await Androulla. Any visions that she had of the future were immaterial. Naming her child, stroking and calling to him through her dreams, she sees, was foolish. The reality is that there was almost something, now there isn't and that is it. But she doesn't know how to put her emotion away if not by lowering it into the ground, or watching it slide on laddered tracks into a furnace.

"This is so much worse," she weeps, into Giannis's neck.

It is so much worse than when she thought she would never conceive.

THE TWELFTH

THE CLINIC HOUSES A door to the edge of life. Not its beginning, Androulla knows by Monday morning, but its end. Stepping in from the rain, she pushes her hood back and drips onto the floor. The waiting room is forensically cold, but she doesn't linger in it. One look at her blanched face and Doctor Constantinou's secretary waves her through.

Before she enters his office, Androulla asks Giannis to wait outside.

His grip on her hand slackens. "You don't want me to be there with you?"

She opens her mouth. Of course she wants him to be with her, always. Except now that her condition is set to turn the examination table into a hospital bed, with a high-pitched whine ringing out as the pulse inside her flatlines and the bed in turn becomes a mortuary table. She wants him to be with her every moment that the news of their baby's death isn't breaking overhead, while his body breaks down inside Androulla's. A word forms on her tongue, then dissolves. She knows what she is going to be told, and how shattering it will be. If she can spare Giannis the direct impact – spare him the horror and the burden of untwining her from the foul odour of his son's end – then she will.

Darkness flashes across his face. Anger, Androulla suspects, for this is his child, too. She squeezes his hand until he drops hers.

"I doubt I'll be long," she says, by way of defence or consolation.

Even as he nods, Giannis looks wounded. The surrounding baby posters tell Androulla she has made the right choice, that he would want to tear their smiling faces from the walls if he accompanied her.

"I'll be here," he says, resigning himself to a low chair.

She mumbles her thanks and goes into the office.

"*Kaliméra*, Androulla *mou*," Doctor Constantinou greets her, sliding a file to one side of his desk.

She shuts the door, diminishing the sounds of feet tapping and phones ringing and keyboards crunching in the reception. There remains the rain at the window, and the gynaecologist's elbows hitting the desk as he laces his fingers to look at her.

"How are you feeling?" he asks.

"Not great," Androulla says, standing over her usual seat.

"You're still in pain? Still bleeding?"

"Yes," she confirms.

"Okay." He unlaces his hands. "Lay down next door and show me your belly."

The examination table has never felt so hard, nor the ultrasound gel so cold. And yet Androulla lies unflinching. She welcomes the press of the transducer into her abdomen as the bringer of closure. None comes. Instead, the gynaecologist leans towards the screen, a murmur snagging between his lips. As she looks up, he turns a knob on the machine. The noise like crickets starts up, and with it Jonah's heartbeat. Androulla's eyes stretch wide.

"Still going strong," Doctor Constantinou marvels, "and the sack is intact."

She nods, breathlessly, looking where he points. Her baby is winking at her from the screen, trying to tell her something, until Doctor Constantinou mutes the sound.

"But it hasn't grown at all." He hangs up his transducer.

Androulla sits upright. "But is he okay? Can we help him?" she frets.

Doctor Constantinou folds the sonogram out of her sight, warning, "Our chances of recovering this are very slim. But we will try. Stay there," he says, sliding open a plastic drawer.

Cleaning herself, Androulla zips up her jeans. She feels like a child with her feet hanging off the side of the table, not touching the floor. Helpless to run and out play with the rain hammering down outside the window, and the orders to roll up her sleeve.

Doctor Constantinou takes hold of her forearm. "What's this?"

"Oh," she says, following his gaze to the pink-white scar beneath her elbow. "That's where I had a cyst removed. Years ago," she adds. Before she knew how many more would shatter inside her.

Doctor Constantinou folds her arm outwards. He dabs the crease of her elbow clean, and she wrinkles her nose at the antiseptic smell.

"Androulla *mou*," he says, in a low voice. "When you go home, I want you to keep taking the pills I wrote you. In the meantime, we'll do a blood test for HCG."

"HCG?" she says.

"Because the embryo is very small," he explains. "The presence of this hormone will tell us, essentially, if the pregnancy is viable."

Androulla doesn't notice the needle until it is pricking her arm. She breathes in as it withdraws, and holds a cotton pad to its entry-point while her blood is bottled. The quantity looks piddling, after what she has lost elsewhere. Doctor Constantinou returns to tape the cotton pad to her skin.

"Go home now and rest. I don't want you to do anything. No dishes, no walking, nothing. Okay?" he says. "Just lay down, drink lots of water, and I'll call you this afternoon with the result."

With her arm stinging, Androulla steps out into the waiting room. Giannis springs from his seat.

When she has paid her thirty euros, he takes her hands. "So?"

"Let's talk outside," she says, as a phone shrills off its hook.

Inside the car, with the rain thrumming down around them, he looks at her.

"He's alive."

"What?"

Androulla turns her head and her raincoat shrieks nylon. "Don't get your hopes up," she says, then touches Giannis's leg. "Sorry. It's just, there is a heartbeat. But it doesn't look good, obviously."

"What can we do?" he asks, taking her hand.

She lifts her shoulders. "Wait."

She tells him about the blood test as they drive home, but says that he is free to do what he wants. He doesn't have to sit with her, anticipating the result.

"I'm not sure I could focus on anything else," he says.

"Me neither."

They hold each other, Androulla expelling every few breaths through gritted teeth with the pain. The rain gives out, leaving the world to hug its knees. Then it is dark, and Androulla cannot be distracted even by the grey sky. She checks that her phone is on loud, time and again.

She sighs. "I'm going to call in half an hour."

"But the doctor will have gone home by then, won't he?" Giannis asks.

"It's not him I need to speak to," she says, hoping this is true.

For it is the out-of-hours midwife she wants, with the voice like stargazing. If it is bad news, Androulla thinks she would prefer it coming from that woman.

It is another one who answers her call, and tells her, coldly, that she should call her doctor's mobile.

Doctor Constantinou answers on the fourth ring. He has called her three times, he says, and left a message. Androulla stares at her phone, on loudspeaker.

"Androulla *mou*, the hormone we were looking for, HCG, it's not present. You have a missed abortion."

She frowns. She thinks, there has been a mistake. She doesn't want an abortion, she hasn't booked and certainly hasn't missed one. But it seems her body instructed this operation, having ruled the baby too small and weak. How wrong it was. Jonah is strong. Despite the pains that the gynaecologist explains are contractions – Androulla has been in labour for days – Jonah is refusing to be born, refusing to die. He is hanging on in his sack outside the realms of both life and death. Briefly, Androulla toys with taking up some inscrutable faith. But she wants her baby to stay in the real, physical world, with her.

"Androulla *mou*," Doctor Constantinou says, gently. "Your body will not change its mind. If the embryo stays there like this, your organs will fail. You will die. You must come and be cleaned."

The Fourteenth

In all her visits to the clinic, it is Androulla's first time ascending the stairs from reception. She leaves her last four-hundred euros and signed waver with Doctor Constantinou's secretary, while his other patients watch with eyes as round as their stomachs. She climbs away from them. She feels that she is climbing away from the world, to a plain beyond the reaches of anything physical as she starves herself. Doctor's orders, today.

Upstairs, the smell of disinfectant is sharp. A nurse with blue plastic wrapped around her every extremity points Androulla to a bin of shoe covers, then leads her with rustling steps to a small, square room.

A man looks up from his wife's bedside. Androulla knows they are married by the bind of their hands, half as old as they are, and by the man's willingness to hunch so close to the source of sweat and urine and staleness in the air. She misses the disinfectant. The nurse leads her through the thick of the must, to a bed separated from its twin only by a thin curtain, and presents her with a dotted gown.

"Take off your clothes," she says, "and put these."

She holds up three more plastic covers, two for Androulla's feet and one for her hair. There is another deluge between her legs.

"You can keep your underwear. For now," the nurse says, and she disappears through the curtain.

Like a schoolgirl getting changed for PE, Androulla unhooks her bra with her top still on. She threads her arms through the sleeves of the hospital gown, and only then drops her trousers. All the while, she can hear the woman beyond the curtain wheezing. Sense her husband praying. Smell her body rotting, even as she struggles on. With what affliction, Androulla cannot say before the nurse asks when the woman started bleeding, and why she didn't come in sooner. The woman's answers come in rasps. Her odour grows fouler, and Androulla lowers her bag of clothes to the floor. She doesn't want to touch her bed, for fear of who else might have festered in it. She loiters instead in the narrow channel between it and a window, whose shutter is most of the way down. The smell of rain is a welcome threat.

"Sit," the nurse bids her, stepping back into view with a clipboard.

Grimacing, Androulla sinks onto the edge of the mattress. It barely gives. Does she have any allergies? the nurse wants to know. Does she smoke? Has she been on medication? Nothing but what the doctor prescribed, Androulla responds. He will be with her soon, the nurse says. He has just one operation to perform before hers. A caesarean.

A contraction seizes Androulla as the nurse withdraws, and she is alone with the pain and the stench of death. She tries to read – a book of short stories by an Irish author – but the words are wasted on her. An hour passes. Then another, and the woman beyond the curtain is sent home. They cannot operate on her when she is bleeding so much, Androulla hears. She ventures from the room to change her sanitary towel.

On her way back she stops, ambushed by the squalling of a newborn baby and the coos of its parents. Doctor Constantinou's congratulations carry down the corridor, and Androulla stares down its windowless length. How can it be that his next delivery will end with hollow footsteps, echoing out of the clinic for a final time? And nothing to carry home but the dull weight of grief. Androulla pulls her gown closer.

Moments later, the nurse leads her to an operating theatre. Androulla balks at the size of the cast. Two girls in surgical masks stand either side of an operating table, surrounded by walls, floor and equipment all as grey as dampened tarmac. A man rattles around the corner with a tray of steel implements, and Doctor Constantinou's voice sounds after him. Androulla steps back, but the nurse who brought her has gone. Instead, one of the new girls approaches.

"I'm still bleeding. A lot," Androulla confides, when the girl asks her to take off her underwear.

"You can lie down first," the girl suggests, indicating the table in the centre of the room.

When she is on her back, trembling, Androulla lifts up her hips and lets the girl strip her. Doctor Constantinou appears and, despite her pain and her fear, Androulla feels an urge to hide the bloody mess between her legs. Then not to. Even for this man, here and now, it is important that she preserves her modesty – and that she does not look prudish. She greets him. For better or worse, she has not completely lost herself.

"*Geiá sas*," sounds the voice of another, shorter man.

He comes into view upside-down, with his mask looking like a hat and a silver trolley dragging alongside him. Androulla cranes sideways to see its flat top and shallow drawers.

"I'm Sotiris. I'll be your anaesthetist." He takes her arm.

As the trolley drawers bang open and shut, Androulla turns her face. She is not afraid of needles, but it is enough to feel the tightening of bands around her arm and the dabbing of chemicals onto her skin. Enough to see everyone else in the room falling still to watch, without doing so herself. When she comes around, she will be one person again, and lonelier than she had ever realised before she became two. But she knows this has to happen, that she cannot be Jonah's mother any more than she can be Kostas's daughter, clinically speaking. She is an only child. Unmarried. Not Cypriot. Just an island of a person, clutching for rafts out of twigs.

At a prick to her elbow crease, she looks up. Sotiris, Doctor Constantinou and the two nurses have gathered as though around a coffin. One of the nurses smiles through her mask.

"You have beautiful eyes," she murmurs.

"Oh. Thank you," Androulla says.

Everyone chuckles, then tapers off into silence. Perhaps with this death will begin a new life, Androulla thinks. Otherwise, what are they waiting for?

Darkness knits inwards from the corners of her vision, while a tingling rises tide-like from her toes. She tilts her chin up to catch a breath, clutching her neck when it burns her throat. It is like being strangled from the inside. Headlights flash before her eyes and she catches Doctor Constantinou's.

"That's normal," he assures her, before the final threads of darkness pull him away.

He is there when Androulla stirs, in the bed that she would not touch earlier. Now, she is tucked in between bars like babies have on their cots. The Holy Mother gazes down from beside a wall-mounted television. Beyond the window, rain patters.

"Rest for an hour," Doctor Constantinou's voice sounds, "and then come and see me. I'll be downstairs."

"*Giatró.*" Androulla reaches after him.

She thinks the rain has drowned out her voice, until the gynaecologist takes her hand.

"Tell me," he says, gently.

She struggles to pull the words through the anaesthetic fog in her brain, and to push them off her weighted tongue. But she needs to know.

"Is it my fault?" Her voice sounds faint. "The hormones I need . . . is it that I can't produce them, or just that I didn't this time? If I got pregnant again . . ."

"Androulla *mou*," Doctor Constantinou says. "You had to run before you could walk with this pregnancy, because it was unplanned. Which, with your condition . . ." He shakes his head. "But you are young. You still have time to catch a baby. When you're ready, we'll check all your levels, everything, and we'll make sure it's a good pregnancy. Okay?"

Androulla nods herself to sleep, the falling rain her lullaby. And when she climbs out of her cot, it is to begin anew.

MARCH

THE FIRST

PERHAPS IT IS THE bar, named for an antidepressant, that tempers Pantelis's usual nervousness. Perhaps it is the deal he has signed with an Athens-based publisher, who found him online.

"I hear congratulations are in order," Giannis says, extending his hand.

With a shrug, Pantelis takes it. "If you can believe it. Thank you, man."

They could be brothers, golden in the light from the bar. Pantelis has his back to its glass front, and a cigarette lodged between his fingers. Androulla looks left to the glass towers of the modern city centre. To her right, cars flash by what remains of the sixteenth-century Venetian Walls, and beyond those the northern border of barbed wire and barrels. A breeze stirs, for the first time this year not scimitar-cold.

She looks back at Pantelis and tuts. "You're too modest."

He embraces her, peering into her eyes as they draw apart.

"How are you doing?" he asks.

She lifts her shoulders. "I've been better."

"Well, I'm glad you could make it. Both of you," he adds, looking to Giannis. He pulls a lighter from his pocket. "I actually haven't been in yet, but you should find a table . . ."

"Thanks. We'll see you in there," Giannis says, guiding Androulla inside by the small of her back.

When she turns her smile forward, it is to light and noise. The word 'dreaming' in neon above a scarred wooden bar. An indiscriminate baseline with bodies bobbing along. And on low sofas in lamplit corners, at squat tables and on rickety chairs, the flashing of pens across pages. Notebooks with their pale innards laid bare, or else hidden behind the cupped hands of their covers as their owners confide self-conscious thoughts. Most are girls with garish hair, silver piercings and tattoos. Boys in un-tucked shirts and worn shoes, with tufts of tobacco falling from the ends of their roll-ups. Like autumn leaves, Androulla thinks. Except that it is spring, and the world is just coming into bloom.

"Where has this place been hiding?" Giannis says, when they reach the bar.

"It's cool, isn't it?" Androulla agrees.

"So, you've been before?" he asks her.

"They did some open mic nights. Last summer," she reminds him.

"Oh," he says.

Tonight, Androulla orders a herbal tea. It comes with a cinnamon stick in a handleless mug, whose finish grates pleasantly under her thumb. Giannis gets a pint.

"Shall we sit there?" he suggests, pointing.

They weave through the crowd to a sticky round table. When Pantelis joins them, it is with another tea.

"You're not drinking?" Giannis asks him.

"Not before I perform," Pantelis says.

"That's brave."

"Are you going to read tonight? Androulla said you were thinking about it . . ."

Giannis takes a swig of beer, coating his top lip in foam.

"Yes." Androulla nods at him. "But he will be drinking first."

"And that's why I don't have a book deal," Giannis says, making a chain of ring marks as he puts his glass down.

They share a laugh.

"Hallo? Hallo?" sounds a voice, in accented English.

A series of taps echoes after it, making Androulla want to dart away like a fish in a tank. She turns her head. Beyond the spiral staircase up to a gallery, and a small table with extra chairs crowded around it, is a microphone stand. A middle-aged woman is standing as though on the verge of falling away from it, wearing a dress that defies both colour and shape and showing her teeth through a gash of lipstick. An invisible hand turns the music down.

"Good evening, everyone. *Kaló apógevma*," the woman says. "I'm Nena, I'll be your host for this evening. Before we get started, I'd like to thank you all for coming–"

There is a rush through the door, a rumbling of 'sorry's and sideways steps as more people crowd inside, taking unlit cigarettes from their mouths. Nena frowns.

"It's just started raining," one girl explains, breathless.

"Hard," a wet-haired boy adds, pulling the door shut behind him.

Laughter ripples.

"Well, now that we're all here," Nena smiles, "could anyone who wants to perform please go to the bar, and write your names on the list . . ."

Her next round of thanks is drowned out by the shunting out of chairs and the urging of friends.

"You should do it," they say to each other, in Greek and English and something else that could be Russian.

"What am I doing?" Giannis asks, as he stands up.

"You'll be great," Androulla assures him. "I believe in you."

She watches him follow Pantelis through the throng of poets and thinkers, then moves to silence her phone.

A text from Naomi. 'Guess who's run a full course of CBT!'

And one from Gary. 'All booked for May', it says, with a screenshot of his ticket from Gatwick Airport to Larnaca.

Androulla's smile broadens. She is proud of her sister. And at last, after a lifetime of her begging him, her father is going to come to Cyprus. He is going to see it and understand her, wholly, for the first time. Sending gushing replies to both messages, she stows her phone back in her pocket.

"Okay," Nena says, resuming her place at the microphone with a clipboard in hand. "Let's welcome our first poet, ladies and gentlemen. Pantelis Efstathiou."

"Oh," Pantelis starts.

He drops his hand from the back of his chair, taking straight to the stage as Giannis sits back down. Androulla keeps her applause up until the lights dim. Her husband shifts closer. Their hands curl together, from the trunks of their forearms to the gnarls of their wrists and the vines of their fingers, every shoot twisting more surely together than the last. Behind them, someone whispers and their companion snickers. Ahead, a spotlight shifts. Adjusting the microphone, Pantelis blinks.

"*Geiá sas*," he greets the room, pulling his phone from his pocket. "So, as Nena said, I'm Pantelis. I'm going to read one poem in Greek and one in English . . . '*Ótan érthei to kalokaíri*'," he introduces the first poem. 'When summer comes'.

Pantelis takes a shaky breath and the room falls still to listen.

"'When summer comes'," he begins.

He could be a mirage through the steam from Androulla's cup. She could be at her laptop as she was last night, doing the research for a new book. Ten days ago, she heard back from the final agent to whom she had submitted 'Copper'. They weren't sure about that story, but they loved her writing. If they took her on, they asked, would she come up with something else?

"'When summer comes . . .'"

Of course, a story inspired by her ordeal with Immigration. Androulla was looking into certain legalities, intending to write a well-informed book, when she discovered it. The dependant's visa is only available to people under twenty-five. She has extended her stay on it this year, but she will not be able to do so again. It is over. She will not get her passport by descent, will not be able to say that she is a Cypriot without the caveats of 'at heart' or 'by adoption'. She will not be able to move forward without first going back to explain to everyone who asks that it is nurture that matters, when it is nature that makes this necessary.

"'When summer comes . . .'"

Pantelis grips the microphone and feedback shrills, making Androulla wince. This afternoon, she closed her laptop and went in search of a present for cousin Christina's baby shower. She ended up in BeBe, the toy shop she had begged to visit every year as a child. Between its packs of hand puppets and the baby dolls whose gawking faces her stepfather used to impersonate, Androulla broke down in tears. The government doesn't care that her earliest memories are here. She is an adult now, with no more child of her own.

"'When summer comes'," Pantelis says, a final time.

He looks more shimmery still through the tears in Androulla's eyes. Giannis squeezes her hand.

"Wife," he whispers.

She looks at him, across the ring-marked table and the haze of cinnamon.

"Will you marry me now?"

"Yes," she says, her heart swelling with the enormity of all they have endured. "I will."

Pantelis ceases to read, and the rain gives way to applause.

Acknowledgements

This book would not exist without my parents, who never asked me to pick a sensible aspiration, or my partner, who never allowed me to. It would not be in print without my friend and cover designer Mark Ecob, whose encouragement has been boundless.

Further thanks go to my editor Miranda Vaughan Jones, a true miracle-worker, and to the friends who have left their marks on this story. You know who you are.

Finally, a thank you to every reader who makes what I do possible. If you enjoyed *Thirty-Eight Days of Rain*, I'd love to read a review! You can find me on Instagram @eva.asprakis, or sign up to hear about new releases on my website.

LOVE AND ONLY WATER

'A delight, and heartbreaking'
Double The Books Magazine

***

'Thought-provoking, sometimes disturbing . . . a beautifully
written story'
Soulla Christodoulou, author of *The Summer Will Come*

***

Can you be whole when your world is in halves?

In the midst of an identity crisis, twenty-one-year-old
Daniela retraces her roots to Cyprus. As whispers resound
through her grandparents' home, she senses their anguish at

Turkey's invasion of The North, still as raw as it was almost fifty years ago. Then her aunt invites her across the border for a picnic.

Beyond the buffer zone she runs into Beyza, who was her girlfriend five years ago when they both lived in London and were from 'the east'. Here and now, with Daniela in The South and Beyza in The North, everything is different.

Faiths conflict. Preconceptions collide. The divided island unravels alongside a war-fractured family. Daniela's is a story of living with uncertainty, and forging an identity as both yet neither.

9 781399 976930